ANOTHER GOOD LOVING BLUES

Another Good Loving Blues

Arthur Flowers

VIKING

yvonne's song

VIKING
Published by the Penguin Group
Viking Penguin, a division of Penguin Books USA Inc.,
375 Hudson Street, New York, New York 10014, U.S.A.
Penguin Books Ltd, 27 Wrights Lane, London W8 5TZ, England
Penguin Books Australia Ltd, Ringwood, Victoria, Australia
Penguin Books Canada Ltd, 10 Alcorn Avenue, Suite 300,
Toronto, Ontario, Canada M4V 3B2
Penguin Books (N.Z.) Ltd, 182–190 Wairau Road,
Auckland 10, New Zealand

Penguin Books Ltd, Registered Offices: Harmondsworth, Middlesex, England

First published in 1993 by Viking Penguin,
a division of Penguin Books USA Inc.

1 3 5 7 9 10 8 6 4 2

LIBRARY OF CONGRESS CATALOGING IN PUBLICATION DATA
Flowers, A. R.
Another good loving blues / by Arthur Flowers.
p.   cm.
ISBN 0–670–84821–2
I. Title.
PS3556.L598A84   1993
813'.54—dc20   92–56715

Printed in the United States of America
Set in Walbaum
Designed by Brian Mulligan

Oluddumare Legba

Open the Gate

CONTENTS

I am Flowers of the delta clan Flowers and the line of O Killens—I am hoodoo, I am griot, I am a man of power. My story is a true story, my words are true words, my lie is a true lie —a fine old delta tale about a mad blues piano player and a Arkansas conjure woman on a hoodoo mission. Lucas Bodeen and Melvira Dupree. Plan to show you how they found the good thing. True love. That once-in-a-lifetime love. Now few folk find the good thing; most folk struggle through life making do—you can learn to love most anybody thats good people. Truth be told its probably best that way because when you find true love my friend its strictly do or die.

My boy Luke Bodeen wasn't even thinking bout no love that bright springly morning he first saw her walking on the dusty little main and only street of Sweetwater Arkansas. But the moment he saw her he wanted her and needed her—she took his breath, she took his heart.

Spring 1918. The Mississippi delta. Bodeen 37 and in his prime. Known to be silver-tongued delta bluesman, Luke Bodeen had left more good women grieving in more towns than he cared to count. But this one touched him. Somewhere deep. Boy didn't know what he was stepping into when he tilted his Stetson just so and crossed her path.

"How do mam, I'm Luke Bodeen. You interested?"

She kept walking, proud little round head cleaving the air. Thick pretty head of hair he couldn't wait to put his fingers into. He matched her stride-for-stride, and their rhythm was a good one. She turned then to look at him and he stumbled into the massive brown galaxies of eyes that saw a mite more than he was comfortable showing.

"A bluesman," he told her, "and a good one too. Outta Memphis Tennessee mostly, but I been around. I come to town with the traveling medicine show."

He paused, poised for an opening.

"Melvira Dupree," she said, "conjure."

He stumbled again. Conjure? Didn't know if he was ready for all that. But he looked her over again and he liked what he saw.

"Well I declare you ain't like no conjure I ever seen."

"Is that so bluesman, and how many have you seen?"

"Oh I seen plenty conjures gal, I'm a well-traveled man, I been to New Orleans, St. Louis and Chicago Illinois, been to New York City, Paris France, Timbucktu and Rio de Janeiro. I done downhome blues wherever the four winds blow. I come back home regular though cause I'm just another good old boy delta born and bred. Warn you up front that I ain't never tossed my shoes under no woman's bed for long. When the blues call I'm liable to answer."

He smiled at her, a bright warm sunny day in the middle of March, a hint of springs to come. She looked him over again with those funny eyes of hers . . . a good spirit, healthy, vigorous . . . she could see that he would be, shall we say, a troublesome man . . . but still . . . there was something about him that spoke to her in that special way. And seeing as she hadn't been any further out of Sweetwater than her traveling spirit had took her, all this talk about getting around intrigued her.

Now Bodeen knew he was being judged, felt her digging. Deep too. Naturally his first urge was to block her, but he found himself just letting her look and hoping she liked what she saw. She, of course, blinked and looked no further—between men and women a degree of mystery is often appropriate.

"I seen hoodoos and conjures of all persuasions," he told her with a downright bodacious grin, "but I ain't

never run across one like you. Don't bother me none
you understand, I'm here to claim you and if you really
conjure, then you know I'm talking true. I likes you gal,
I likes your style, really truly I do."

He offered his arm and a big old country courting
smile.

She laughed with a newfound pleasure and took
them both. Most of the men in Sweetwater were afraid
to talk to the woman in her.

"You ain't half bad yourself bluesman."

Her throaty voice was a tickle, a challenge, a music
that bewitched him. He preened under her obvious approval like a old bantam rooster and commenced to sang
himself a brand-new blues.

I'll bring you sweet southern loving
in a old tin cup
pour it on your body baby
then I'ma lap it all up
everyday
Show you how much I love being your man.

"Gon git you too," he sang, "gon git you good, cause
I don't mind working at it."

She just as tickled as she can be.

"Do tell . . . bluesman."

They stopped in front of the Sweetwater General
Store and she rested her hand lightly on his arm.

"I thank you for your company Mr. Bodeen, you are
kinda cute."

"O I'm a lot more than cute. As you shall see when
I come a courting. Course I ain't gon pester you none

just now, though. Just enough to put me on your mind some."

She went inside, laughing pertly over a curved brown shoulder bare to the sun.

"You don't know you want to be on my mind bluesman."

"Oh yes I do," he sang after her. "I ain't scared of no conjure, what you gon do, hoodoo a man the blues already claim? I'll be seeing you around Miz Melvira Dupree."

Now it would be safe to say that the good coloredfolk of Sweetwater Arkansas were scandalized and mystified when their conjure woman took up with that blues-singer, when he stayed on after the medicine show left town and moved into her little place out there on Sweet-water Creek.

The local lads were understandably upset with him. They wouldn't have minded a chance with that fox Du-pree, but she was known to have a temper, and any old fool know that courting a conjure woman with a temper is a chancy thing. The two of them bickered and fought about as much as they laughed and loved, always mad at each other about something. Any day now folks expected to see that boy hopping round like a toadfrog or wiggling on his belly like a snake. But whatever he was doing, he was doing it right. Melvira Dupree changed up on them. She walk down the street smiling at folks and greeting them good morning just like a regular neighbor. But it was when she started hanging out down at the local jukejoint where Lucas got a job barrellhousing every Friday and Saturday night that folks really commence to commenting. Girl started flouncing that big impressive boodie of hers and having herself much too good of a time for the puritans from the old school, who couldn't quite recall a conjure woman quite like this one. Of course the older Sweetwater women, elders all who didn't miss very much, would poke each others ribs when they saw her walking around town glowing. They knew a recently satisfied woman when they saw one. After all a good man is still hard to find and even conjures appreciate good loving.

And that boy Bodeen, he just as snug as a hog in fresh summer mud. When he wasn't all knotted up mad at her, he could be seen walking around with his thumbs hooked in those red suspenders and grinning proud as a brand-new fool.

Scandalized as they were at their conjure lady taking up with a bluessinger, of all things, you could tell he loved that woman something truly fierce. A buncha Sweetwater women like the way his lean brown fingers caressed music out of those cold piano keys and wondered what music he coaxed from a woman's warm body, but he went home to Melvira Dupree each and every night. Took his money home each and every week, too, like a natchural man, and wasn't never fool enough to try and raise up his hands against her. They did fuss a lot, but folks come to decide that they just liked to fuss.

So the good coloredfolk of Sweetwater Arkansas gave their grudging approval. To this day Sweetwater folk are known for being bighearted, and there just ain't no counting for a conjure's taste noway.

Course what folks saw from the vantage points of their big wraparound porches wasn't the whole story. Never is. Any good story is always at least 4 or 5 stories deep. And since this is a good story, I expect you to pay close attention to the weave of it. Even they couldn't tell the whole story. But what they did come to understand deep down in once starved and lonely souls, is that when you do find yourself some of that real good loving, if you got any sense at all, you hold on to it.

Truth. I swear by all thats holy.

On
the
Nature

of
Sweetwater
Loving

Blues and women. Women and the blues. According to Lucas Bodeen they come together. The best women to come through a man's life always leave a good blues behind, and Melvira Dupree was the best woman Luke Bodeen ever had. Taught him the best blues he ever sang, you don't know you need it till you've had it and you don't miss it till its gone. It's an old

old song, and Melvira Dupree was the one taught him how to sing it right. Moved in with her out of laziness more than anything else. Always been more comfortable with a woman than without, and she was the one available at that time and place. Simple as that. Even back then he knew she was strange, even more so than women are by nature. But he soon found she had a way with him like no other woman before. She made him feel. She bothered him. Bothered him real bad. Long as he was with her he kept saying that he was just passing through. But a year later he was still there and still comfortable. Satisfied. He likes to think that she was too. Till the rooster crowed.

It was early one morning in the Sweetwater Woods. They were out gathering herbs, specifically Life Everlasting. She always gathered in morning, said morning was best for the earth's medicine. "The earth is stronger then."

Hoodoo talk.

This particular morning he was supposed to be showing her this big batch of Life Everlasting that he had seen when cutting through the woods the other day. He had told her about it because he knew she was always on the lookout for Life Everlasting, and she used it enough for him to know it when he saw it.

It was early on a pretty morning. The woods were a wet and sparkly green and Bodeen was kinda feeling the morning in his soul. He's listening to earlymorning birdsong and he's wondering what blues birds sing. He started whistling, called himself mimicking birdblues about hungry hawks and slithering snakes, about warm southern winds and the fuzzy little feathers that line a she-bird's neck. And what about that first time in flight? Thats got to be nice. A windy blues. Eyes slitting lazily, his arms in front of him, he played with the fingering. Classic air piano.

"Bodeen." Melvira cleared her throat, half amused, half irritated, "my Life Everlasting?"

It took him a minute to focus; right, Life Everlasting. He looked around until he recognized where he was and smiled for effect. "This way for sure, right over the hill here."

They crested the hill and saw the bush below—Life Everlasting. She was pleased. She had been none too sure he knew what he was talking about. She smiled, and when Melvira Dupree smiles the sun beams, flowers bloom and every tree in Tennessee glows crimson with pleasure.

She kissed his jaw, rubbing her lips lightly across the morning stubble. "Bless you Bodeen, that's the finest batch of Life Everlasting I ever seen."

She was singing now, every word a song. She did it all the time, everything she said she sang, thats just the way she spoke, but when she was happy or pleased it really got bad, she could sing the stars out of the sky just by calling out their names. So he's real contented, watching her scramble down the hill, wild mane of her hair billowing out behind her. He's feeling kinda playful and so while she's stuffing Life Everlasting into her burlap tote bag, he ducked off behind a big gnarly oak beside her. He plucked him some little yellow flowers and called himself gon surprise her. Get that, surprise a conjure woman. She was looking dead at him when he stepped out, flowers in hand.

"Thought I'd pick some herbs too," he said. She knew what he was about. Some of that earlymorning sun-kissed loving. She took his flowers from him and looked at them disdainfully. "These are flowers Bodeen, not herbs. What am I supposed to do with flowers?"

He acted like he's offended and reached for them. She snatched them away and popped him across the face. Bright yellow petals explode around his head.

She laughed and darted out of range when he reached for her. "Come back here you."

She darted behind the trunk of that oak behind her and he chased her around it. "Lucas Bodeen you cut it out you hear? Don't you make me drop my Life Everlasting."

She stopped and glared. Pure bluff.

"I'm warning you Bodeen, I'm gonna . . ."

He grabbed. She evaded. Just barely.

"Warning me what? Told you about trying to hoodoo a man the blues already claim."

She laughed. "You mighty sure of yourself ain't you bluesman?"

"Only cause that's the way you like it."

She was laughing so hard he almost caught her. She laughed so rarely. Melvira Dupree was one of those rigid folks that take life strictly serious. Fun had to sneak up and prove itself far as Melvira Dupree was concerned. Bodeen, he was a playful man, make a laugh out of any old thing, good times and bad. Blues training. A magic she found hard to resist. He snatched at her and she stumbled getting away.

"Yeah," she said from the other side of the tree, "I like my men manly, but you way too cocky, I oughta try you boy."

"Try me now whydoncha?"

He grabbed her, "I gotcha now" and, giggling, they tumbled to the ground. Her body writhed with laughter and the effort of evading him, and suddenly she was just laying there, her eyes locking his, her fingers snaking behind his neck and pulling him down onto her parted lips. Sweet lips fresh like they never been kissed. He gave up real quick, letting himself just melt onto her body, when suddenly she flipped him over and she was on top.

"Who got who?" she breathed into the hollow of his throat, and then her tongue was deep in his mouth and her dress was down around her hips when like it was right in his ear he heard a rooster crow, echoes floating through the trees and hanging in the crisp morning air like a old delta fieldholler. Firm tittymeat in his hand, fat growing nipple in his mouth, you know he wasn't hardly paying no attention to no rooster crowing. Till he felt her distraction. Her body went limp and he looked up at her face. She was listening to the echoes of the rooster with a unfocused gaze that he recognized. Another damned sign. Living with a hoodoo ain't easy. Looked to him sometimes like everything was a sign with this woman. Everything that happened anywhere in the world meant something. Though what a rooster crowing at six a.m. said beyond Good Morning was beyond him.

He didn't say anything while she pulled loose and rose, brow wrinkled and eyes all out of focus. She pulled her dress up and kissed him absently. "Gotta go Bodeen. Okay?"

He nodded, lucky to get that much. By now he knows better than to question a Sign, so he just laid there with his hands behind his head and watched her dress, thick black hair tangled and laced with leaves and twigs. Strange strange woman this woman of his, he thought, wonder why I always choose the strange ones, seemed like I'da learned by now.

She strided off through the woods and he watched her go. Erect and proud and smooth like young midnight. A force. His. He had to smile. A helluva woman that answers to me. I like that. Always did.

"Why did she leave me?"

The old woman looked at Melvira with eyes that missed nothing. Her frail little body was lost in the deep folds of an old overstuffed high-backed chair. Her broad mahogany features were weathered into agelines as rough as the bark on the oldest tree in the forest. She smelled old, ancient, slow. She wasn't, though, as old as she looked. Wore age like a garment, the mask of a elderly little lady just another trick that only the black-bullet eyes gave away. Hoodoo Maggie. Outside the little one-room shack behind the Sweetwater General Store, the town was coming to life. A dog barked. The cats ignored it. Seven of them, all over the little room, climbing in Maggie's lap, brushing against Melvira's calves, digging at the bag of Life Everlasting at Melvira's feet.

"Heard from her finally have you?"

They stared at each other for long moments before Melvira dropped her eyes.

"You ain't ready to try me yet child." Maggie chuckled, her breath scented with years of chewed tobacco. A silky haired gray jumped in Maggie's lap and she absently scratched it behind the ears. She sucked a tooth, a habit of emphasis. "Phwwt, I didn't teach you enough to try me, you remember that. I'll let you know when you ready."

Melvira's eyes snapped up, a child's defiance. The old woman had raised her. Melvira's earliest memories are of Maggie and chewing tobacco. Cats & jars & potions & plants stacked in every corner. Drying herbs hanging in bundles from every rafter. Behind Maggie, dried snake skin hung from a corner post. The walls were papered with old yellowing newsprint. Part of Melvira's duties as a child had been to read the brittle newsprint to the old lady when her sight went bad. Melvira had grown up here. Her, Hoodoo Maggie and seven cats. Always seven. All that she knew of the hoodoo way she had learned from Hoodoo Maggie. Yet she and Maggie had never been close, a hard uncrossable distance between them that caused Melvira to leave when she was 15, full grown and already a known hoodoo. Since then Melvira had come calling once a month, precisely once, business, obligation, habit, ritual, never stayed long. Didn't much care for being reminded of her childhood alone, a strange little pigtailed girl whose days were spent squirming as Hoodoo Maggie drilled her with the lore of herbs and the powers of earth, air, fire, water and the mojo. Had dragged her in tow to her daily consultations. Taught her how to read sign, how to see, to know, to command the spirits. Taught her how to conjure reality from secrets, words and dreams, taught her the true names of gods and things. Taught her the magics of love and hate and the human passions. Lessons lessons lessons, while all around them life scampered happily by playing ring-around-the-rosie and hide-and-seek, everybody in the world having fun, living life, everybody but little Melvira Dupree. Even then she had known she was special, but she would have traded it all for one friend.

Melvira looked away. "Who is she Maggie, why did she leave me?" Her voice was sad and broken.

The old woman looked out of the depths of her overstuffed chair through eyes suddenly and unexpectedly soft.

"Woman with your power ought to know," she muttered. Jealousy painted the air faintly of cinnamon.

"Who is she?"

"Strange you never asked before."

"Strange you never told me."

Maggie shrugged; she saw no reason to indulge Melvira's resentments, and pointed, "Oshun, fetch." The silky gray in her lap jumped gracefully down and padded softly over to a pile of redflanneled sacks lying haphazardly in a corner. Tail twitching, the big cat used her teeth to drag one over to Hoodoo Maggie's bare feet.

"Good girl." Maggie took the hand from the gray and looked it over, weighing it in her hand.

"Phwwt," she sucked, "woman needs children."

"You didn't." Melvira said coldly, "She didn't."

Effie Dupree. The name floated unbidden into Melvira's mind. Effie Dupree. Melvira worked her mouth to rid it of a sudden sourness. Melvira knew little of the woman who was supposed to be her mother. Rumors mostly, a known hoodoo of some power, come to town with her belly already big, stayed long enough to have Melvira and leave her with the town crazy woman. As a child, Melvira Dupree had wasted many a lonely little girl's starlight, starbright, first star I see tonight wishing a faint memory to life, seeking refuge from a looming life as a stranger in this world. The woman never came, and the child had banished even the memory from her mind. Till the dreams began. Till a rooster crowed in the Sweetwater Woods.

"Who is she Maggie, why did she leave me here?"

Maggie looked at Melvira with a uneasiness totally alien to her. When she spoke, her voice was more the soft caress of Melvira's childhood, before Melvira came into her own.

"Effie Dupree was a powerful hard woman to know." She said finally, "As to why she left you with me she didn't say."

"And you just took me, just like that."

"Hard to deny Effie Dupree anything she wanted."

Melvira desperately needed to know more but was unable to ask. She sat rigid with need. Her rigidity brought a smile to Maggie's thin lips. She sighed and something hard inside her fell away.

"Can't say I ain't thought about it some," she said, "specially when you'd aggravate me. I knew she wanted me to teach you what I know. Phwwwt. Shango knows

I didn't expect to be stuck with you this long. Taught you everything I know though, mostly, raised you best I could." The old woman paused and shifted into a more comfortable position in the depths of the big chair. "Never did like you though."

Melvira knew, she had always known, it meant nothing to hear it said.

"I'll never be what you are," the old woman said.

"I'm not . . ." started Melvira.

"Yes you are," said Maggie. "Don't do to fight your destiny chile. You been chose."

Melvira's face composed itself. This was an old argument.

"I don't want . . ."

Hoodoo Maggie interrupted her impatiently. "Phwwt, honey the power don't care what you want. The gods chose who they want to do their work and thats that. You deny it and it'll hurt you, I ain't telling you nothing you don't know." She fingered the redflannel bag in her hand. "You do well to have your fun while you can. Your fate be under lock and key one day."

Melvira looked away. Maggie reached out a fragile little parchment-thin hand and touched her arm with a rusty affection.

"You be careful now girl, love do funny things to a hoodoo. A little pleasuring now and then you can control that, but love is something else altogether. Don't know love do for a hoodoo child."

Melvira shrugged off her hand and started to leave.

"Don't forget your roots chile."

A redflannel bag in an open palm. Melvira went back

for it, thanked her with a calculated nod and turned away.

"Melvira."

Melvira stopped at the door without turning. Didn't bother Maggie, she was used to talking to Melvira's back. Way too stiff for a hoodoo chile, Maggie thought sourly, good wind would blow her over.

"Any woman," she told the stiff back, "that would tear her own right eye out of her own head wouldn't hesitate to tear her child from her womb."

Melvira left behind her the sound of Maggie's raucous laughter and a gasped mutter barely heard, "And they call me crazy."

Usually Melvira walked through the woods as a natural and valued part of them. She crushed none of the small creatures that crawled the ground beneath her feet, she broke no twigs in passing, she left no crushed flowers in her wake. Usually Melvira savored mornings, earth's breath still fresh and uncluttered. But today she is preoccupied with a one-eyed woman that haunts her dreams, and her passage through the Sweetwater Woods is stiff and unheeding. Today she is an intruder. A rooster's call bounces hollow echoes off the trees.

How dare she rise from the grave?

Melvira walked with a purpose that soon brought her to a shadowed glade dappled with determined sunlight. A mighty oak dominated it, its great leafy canopy rustling with pleasure at her approach and casting its shade out to greet her. Only now aware of the rages that raced her blood through her veins, Melvira settled her back against the rough trunk.

"Your first door," Maggie had told her, "Legba's gift."

It had been months before the little pigtailed child was able to get through. Now she reached out, and in the beat of a human heart she knew the calm serenity that only the elder trees know.

Will you go?

The question is heavy with the weight of years. Oak is a ponderous, often pompous clan. Melvira answered before the question was fully formed.

What does she want?

You.

Why now, after all these years? She's wanted nothing to do with me before.

Melvira Dupree was mad. She detected Old Oak's amusement and it made her madder still. Sensing a quest in the making, Old Oak's leaves rustled with pleasure. This would be a good trade piece. Rooted like they are, trees are notorious gossips, constantly trading rumors and memories like hoarded jewels around the world from tree to tree. They care little about the truth of their tales, knowing as they do that there are many truths and to exist, if only in rumor, speaks for itself. A tree's wealth is counted in knowledge, and it is said that on a mountaintop in the Southern Sudan lives a wise old baobab that knows all there is to know.

Usually Melvira finds Old Oak's bluntness satisfying, but today she doesn't care for the frankness that comes so natural to the elder rooted ones who know decades and even centuries as fleeting ephemeral things. Human skin is a bit more sensitive than bark, and even conjures must sometimes hide from the truth.

She is still your mother.

She been no mother to me. She is nothing to me.

All that you are is because of her. You are her greatest work.

Melvira had never in her life known such fury. Headache fury. She stood and stalked off snarling, leaves trembling in her wake.

I owe her nothing.

Melvira needed him close and she wanted him now. It'd be safe to say Bodeen didn't put up much of a fight when she came home and came at him, smooth brown skin glowing with desire. She pulled him hard into her, and the furious tension that had ridden her home carried her whimpering into the growing moment. The world around them faded away and only they existed. Warm and snug and satisfied, Bodeen thought contentedly just how good she feels to him, how just right she fits him, and in the moment, in the fine and singular moment, Bodeen felt so good he thought surely this must be how the good Lord intended for man to live.

"What you laughing about Bodeen?" she gasped, satiated and at peace, stroking his still heaving chest with her fingertips, waiting for her heart to quit pounding in her ears.

"Was just thinking," said Bodeen, deliciously limp, flat on his back with his arms splayed out. "This must be how the good Lord intended for man to live."

"Woman too," she said as she licked his nipple, "woman too."

Oh my strange strange stangaree baby
Just as strange as she can be . . .

Under a moon like a big bright hole in the midnight sky, the little jukejoint down at the crossroads was a weaving and a swaying, goodtiming coloredfolk flocking from miles around cause Lucas Bodeen was throwing down. That new blues of his. Sweet Stangaree Baby. So down and dirty that everytime he hit a chord the piano would jump off the floor a foot or so. If I'm lying I'm flying. A full foot.

But when she love me, oh how she love me
cant nobody love me like my stangaree do
my strange strange stangaree baby
you sweet sweet stangaree you

Course there are those that say the juke wasn't actually swaying as claimed, narrow-minded folks that's strict to the letter of the law. But even they don't question the fact that Lucas Bodeen played piano from way down deep that night. An inspired stangaree blues spreading through the juke like the Big Muddy flooding the lowlands. Bodeen was feeling good and his blues were feeling even better. The little jukejoint at the crossroads may not have actually been swaying, but it was thoroughly alive with folk sweating off a long hard week in the fields and farms of Sweetwater Arkansas.

"Git it Bodeen," said Jake, putting his guitar down

and sitting back in his chair to listen. "I guess tonight belong to you brother. Stangaree on down."

But he couldn't help himself. He jumped right back in. Guitar talking. Jake was Bodeen's blues partner. A guitar playing fool born and bred in Sweetwater. Young-boy, the kind of kid brother Bodeen would have always liked to have had. One of those folks you get to know so easy its like you grew up together. They played a strong blues, talked much trash, and just loved to cut head. Going up against each other like that kept em both sharp and growing. Nice to have a buddy that challenge you to your best, only kind worth having. Like BB & Bobby. Martin & Malcolm. Ishmael & Amiri. DorisJean & Ter-rymac. Far as Bodeen was concerned, they raised some mighty fine folks down here in Sweetwater Arkansas. He had found himself a good woman and a blues partner, couldn't ask for more than that out of no town.

Jake started soloing. It got good to him and he com-mence to hopping around on one leg while he played. The juke roared. Homeboy had style. Bodeen leaned back and emptied the glass of brown Tennessee sipping whiskey he always kept on the end of his piano. With his right hand still playing the blues, he motioned with his left for a refill. Big Pig Willie—owner, bartender and bouncer—brought it right over. It was common knowl-edge that a well-lubricated Lucas Bodeen was a blues-playing fool. Bodeen took a long drink while still work-ing his right hand on the keys until Jake ran out of steam.

"Whooeeee Bodeen," said Jake, pulling the strap of his guitar over his head and wiping his face with a pocket handkerchief. "If that's the way you play with stiffed up fingers I hate to contest you at your best. Those musta been some of those St. Louis licks you been telling me about. When you gon show me how to do it like they do it upriver?"

Jake had learned most of his licks from asking folks that came through. Never had the urge to wander like a lot of delta bluesmen. Delta bluesmen were known for traveling—river, road and rail. Calling theyself being free. Most blackfolk in the delta was indentured to their whitefolk. Might as well a been slaves, unable to leave the sharecropped land, the millgang, the weekly paycheck, the company store debt. Somefolk, though, was of a notion to take off on their own, letting the blues pay their way and spreading em like spores in the wind. Course now this legion of traveling bluesmen weren't considered stable members of the community. Folks appreciate a good blues anywhere, but they never did love those traveling bluesmen like they did their locals—the ones that stayed home and raised families and could probably play you a gospelsong as quick as a blues. Rouse the same folk with either. Jake was one of those. Hard-working young man. Pride of the community. Brought him up a yearly crop and seven kids. Swore he was still courting his wife. Wasn't no reason not to believe him either, she had that satisfied look about her. And the boy still found time to beg every bluesman that came through Sweetwater for instruction. That old boy loved that old guitar of his as much as he loved his woman. He handled it constantly, stroking the neck, strumming chords while he talked.

"I'll show you those licks when you ready boy," said Bodeen.

"I was born ready old man."

"Old man?" snorted 37-and-in-his-prime Bodeen. He quickly rumbled through some chords so lowdown Jake had to scramble to catch up.

Oh she such a hardheaded woman
just as hardheaded as she can be . . .

"You best not to let Melvira hear you talking about her like that," laughed Jake.

"Ain't necessarily about Melvira, just a song."

"Yeah, okay just a song. Treat me like I don't know nothing about the blues."

Bodeen shrugged it off. No way Lucas Bodeen was going to let how somebody feel about it stop him from doing a good blues. Be real. He strutted his bass with his left hand, pointing with his right over the top of his piano. "You got a lot to learn about handling women youngster, bout as much as you got to learn about playing the blues."

"Might be so," said Jake, bottletop sliding, "but I'm old enough to know a good thing when I see it. That woman of yours is a good thing."

"Knowing it when you see it is not the same as getting and holding it. I got her, you ain't."

"I got my own, I'm just saying to you that lotsa folks round these parts wouldn't mind having that woman of yourn."

Bodeen sighed and looked to the heavens. "I'm Luke Bodeen youngster and I'm from the old school. Be damned if I got to worry about having a woman took from me."

"Whoa up hoss," said Jake, holding his hands up and

letting his guitar dangle from his neck. "I'm just calling it like I see it. I'ma bluesman too. I got a right to the truth."

Bodeen snorted. "Ha. You ain't no bluesman yet. A bluesbaby maybe. You spend more time playing the blues and less time trying to tell grown folk they business, you might make something of yourself one day."

Jake replied with flying chords; Bodeen stepped on them and they were off again, cutting head and talking trash till the sun rose and closed up shop. Outside, the gray delta morning was crisp, and Bodeen put his collar up.

"Come in a little early next Friday and we can work on that St. Louis crosslick."

"Nine o'clock okay?"

No, nine o'clock was not okay, Bodeen started to say. They didn't hit till ten and he had been thinking something more like 15 minutes, but what could he do? Couldn't begrudge a young man no learning. Boy reminded him of himself when he was a youngster, trying to get it all done in a day. They split at the crossroads, two generations of the blues.

Bodeen was almost home when off in the distance a passing freight train wailed at the morning. He stopped to listen. The thought hit him that he had been here in Sweetwater Arkansas a whole year now. Long time to have stayed in any one town. He worked fingers stiff with a long night. Time get away from you if you ain't careful. Specially a man that lived as hard as Lucas Bodeen. Bet they were playing some new licks back on the river. Down Memphis, New Orleans, St. Louis, Chicago way.

He probably falling behind. Somebody somewhere was doing a better blues. The sun peeked over the horizon and outlined their little place by the creek in muted shades of orange. He thought about that warm bed and the even warmer woman lying there. A damn good woman, Melvira Dupree. He pulled the collar of his coat up around his neck and hurried some. She liked to sleep on her back, arms thrown over her head. His sweet stangaree baby. Hated to hurt her, but in the final analysis he was longrail delta bluesman and one day it would be time to go. Thats just the way it is. He had to be where the blues was. Far as Lucas Bodeen was concerned, that was the whole point in living. That lonesome earlymorning wail came again, further on down the road, fainter now, soft and muted. The 6:45 to Memphis. Running late.

Candles flicker at the four corners of the earth. Melvira Dupree sits quietly in an old cane-back rocking chair. She is earth still, her eyes closed. Suddenly they twitched behind her eyelids, and her traveling spirit moaned, that haunting melancholy whimper of a traveling spirit in trouble. She called it back. Quickly. A traveling spirit too far from home draws predators like a victim bleeding in shark-filled waters. After a moment her eyes open and the rocker starts again, slowly back and forth, gradually building up to a steady and irritated beat. Effie Dupree lives. That much she knows. It is knowledge that restores neither calm nor balance. The dreams come. The rooster crows. Yet the door remains closed. Knowledge is denied.

Melvira Dupree was considered by folk in these parts of Arkansas to be a somewhat unconventional conjuror. First off she was such an attractive woman. Folks had very clear-cut ideas of what a conjure should look like: strange, weird and otherworldly. Second off, she was living in sin with a bluesman. Folks expected more decorum from their conjurors. But she was good. Folk'll forgive you anything if you good. Hoodoo Maggie had taught her well and at 32 she has never been defeated. Life ain't touched her. Consequently, she was partial to her right hand over her left—folks that wanted to put a trick on somebody went to Hoodoo Maggie. They come to Miz Melvira to have the trick took off. Could find your lost items, lost mates, lost health. Told old man Cratchet where to find that lost deed of his and saved him from losing his farm. Told that fool Rooster Clay where his cows was that time. The sheriff over at Clarksville ask her her opinion on a case in a minute, felony or misdemeanor it don't matter. Why just last year she restored the feeling in Janet Gibson's legs after the doctors told her she would never walk again. You name it, Melvira Dupree could fix it. Treated Sweetwater Arkansas like it belonged to her personal, a spider in the middle of her web, responding to every twitch and shimmer, a community resource that belonged to the good colored-folk of Sweetwater Arkansas like the lumber in the Sweetwater Woods or the catfish in Sweetwater Creek. Knew most everybody's secrets and all their business, and didn't have no shame about interfering as she saw fit. Queen Ester knew she was in for a lecture before she came. A small woman made even smaller for her determination to be overlooked by life, Queen Ester hid herself in the ritual of living, avoiding whenever possible its mess and its glory. So good at it that even Melvira was surprised when Queen Ester came to her with brand-new life exuding from her every pore.

"Should have come to see me before," grumbled Melvira Dupree, "not after."

Queen Ester sighed with all the weariness that the human race was capable of. All her life she had been late. Or something. As if fearing that Melvira would refuse her, she took a deep breath and rushed her plea out in one gasp.

"All I want is something to kill his seed Miz Melvira, don't want him, don't want his memory."

Candles flicker at the four corners of the earth. Shadows dance. Melvira looked at Queen Ester till the woman dropped her head, her confidence quickly seeping out of her.

"What you really want child?"

Queen Ester bowed her head. "I probably wants him back Miz Dupree."

Soft, almost unheard. Dupree's expression clearly asked Why? Young Jubal was a known roustabout.

"Ain't no why Miss Dupree, just want him back. Don't wanna live without him."

Now Melvira was a hoodoo after all and peoples passions was her business. But she didn't approve. The flickering candles make the frown on her face sterner than it is, and Queen Ester's hard-worn audacity completely collapsed.

Melvira took out her Johnny Conquer roots. She

touched the fisted roots to Queen Ester's forehead before dropping them to the table. She stared at the design long moments before repeating the sequence. Seeking secrets. Finally she looked up. Tired. Surprised. Looking deeply at Queen Ester in an attempt to further see what lay beneath the meek surface. She never would have expected Family. Even with Struggle.

And then in the distance they heard the faint echoes of a rooster. Melvira listened. She seemed to forget that the woman was still sitting there in front of her. It was long moments before Queen Ester ventured to speak.

"Miss Melvira?"

Melvira didn't respond.

"Miss Melvira?"

Melvira's eyes refocused; Queen Ester felt her return.

"You can have him," Melvira said crisply. "Take flowers and honey to the creek. Leave them for the spirits. You take this here candle, you burn it a half hour fore sunrise everyday till Sunday next. You sit there with that candle and you think about this. Let the sun cut through that fog in your mind and if you still decide you want him, I'll give him to you. The spirits say you can have him."

Queen Ester hesitated.

"Don't you worry none," said Melvira, "my working is the sun and the moon and all the stars. You rest easy. Melvira Dupree is working on you."

Mary Ellen Rogers was known to be a no-nonsense woman, practical, down to earth, Capricorn sun moon and rising, respected elder of the Sweetwater New Zion Baptist Church and long past child-bearing age when she had Carolee. "God's Gift," Mary Ellen called her when she was alone with the equally proud Willie Bob. Willie Bob was a real quiet man mostly, hardly ever smiled except when that baby was around. Both of them felt just as blessed as they could be. Mary Ellen breasted that baby as long as she could and felt in some way inadequate when her laughing little two-year-old suddenly quit laughing and took to her bed without being told, hot and fevered and spitting black mucus. A worried Mary Ellen and Willie Bob were still up about two a.m. when they heard a knock on the door. Willie Bob opened it and stepped back. Melvira Dupree stood on the porch, shoulder-draped white shawls gleaming haintlike in the darkness. Melvira motioned the gaunt woman to step outside, and Mary Ellen's breath caught in her throat. Clearly concerned, Willie Bob stood uncertainly in the doorway, a shaft of light from inside throwing his shadow on the two women standing on the porch. Melvira Dupree touched Mary Ellen's shoulder, and Mary Ellen instinctively jerked away. Melvira pointed to the west.

"There's a city there," she said.

"Little Rock?"

"No. A city of the dead."

"Oh," said Mary Ellen, little voice breaking, "the cemetery."

"Call someone you know there."

"Wha? But . . ." She looked at the rigid figure beside her.

"Call!"

Hard, angry.

"My friend Sally."

"Call her."

"Sally." A dry whisper.

Melvira watched the night. Mary Ellen stood quietly beside her, watching Melvira Dupree and listening to Carolee's faint whimpers from inside the house.

Melvira caught her breath.

"Call another."

"Another?"

"Quickly!" she said in a voice like cold hard steel.

"My grandmother?"

"Call her!"

"Pearl."

"Again."

"Pearl."

Inside Carolee stopped whimpering, and the night was suddenly still. Melvira redraped her shawls and left the porch. Mary Ellen went inside. Carolee wore the faint smile of a peaceful sleep. Praise the Lord. The next day Willie Bob left a mess of greens, yams and mason-jarred preserves at the door of the little cabin on Sweet-water Creek.

There's a man going round
and he's taking names.

It was a hot jukejoint June night that the crooked old man in black came. The night was most over, the few folks still on the dance floor were moving slow and easy in a dim smoky room like a morning halfdream, dawn still an unborn promise in the east. Big Pig Willie came from behind the bar and opened the front door of the juke to let a cool breeze float through.

Melvira was one of the stragglers, sitting at a table with Geneva, waiting on Bodeen mostly. Bodeen and Jake were on stage, doing their favorite blues, Going Down Slow, I've had my fun if I don't get well no more.

Melvira appreciated the cool breeze coming in through the open door, and she and Geneva were sharing a mellow earlymorning laugh when the crooked old man walked in. She felt him enter and looked up. A bigheaded man in black shades, lean and bent, curiously dignified and correct in a hightop silk hat and a black boxtailed evening coat. The few dancers left on the floor apparently neither saw nor touched him, dancing around him as if he were an empty space. His dark glasses glittered in the halflit club and smoke rose lazily from a cigar in his mouth. The Baron himself. The music drew his attention, and his head slowly swiveled to the stage. Jake and Bodeen. For the first time in her life Melvira knew a fear so deep it left her weak.

"No," she whispered fiercely, her eyes narrowing into vicious feline hunting slits, "no!"

The Baron stumbled and choked on his cigar. More surprised than angry, he swiveled his oversized head. A steady hand lifted dark glasses and their eyes locked. Melvira was suddenly dizzy, the crowded juke wavering out of focus. Another world. The noose was suddenly loosened and she was left discombobulated.

The flat black eyes issued a casual, almost amused command and, choking back a cry, Melvira fled from the juke into the growing morning. Bodeen missed a chord. He frowned, thick eyebrows drawing together in his forehead. But he hadn't noticed anything out of place so he shrugged it off. He played on.

The Baron watched her leave before turning back to the stage with a rather tired and weary sigh. Everybody got burdens to bear.

Jake and Bodeen took a break. Bodeen took a drink of the Tennessee sipping whiskey on the edge of his piano top and worked his stiff fingers. He looked at them with disgust. They bothered him whenever it rained or on chilly nights. The bones going bad, Melvira had told him. One day they'd go out on him. What would he do when he couldn't play the blues no more? The crooked old man in the black shades and a silk tophat walked toward the stage. Jake noticed him then and watched him approach with snake-eyed fascination. Like they the only two people in the juke. In the whole world. Already? thought Jake. He knew immediately. You always do. Sometimes its worth your while to fight and sometimes it ain't. Jake calculated it right away, staring at his reflection in the black shades and seeing the flat "no" there. And he saw all the things he hadn't done, the women he hadn't loved, the blues he hadn't sung. The children unborn. He shook his head and he whispered, "Why me God? Why me?"

"Hello bluesman."

The Baron's voice is a dry dry wind and Jake smiles a deep and enigmatic shrug of a smile. He had forgot hadn't he. He was a bluesman wasn't he. Suddenly mellow, he held out an arresting hand. The crooked old man hesitated, and Jake caressed the neck of his guitar. He

had picked a lot of cotton to buy that old guitar of his,
hands so callused it was sometimes hard to feel the
music through them. I spec it was worth it, he had no
complaints. He had had his fun if he didn't get well no
more. If he got to go down he was gon go down slow.
Jake smiled and began to play, a beautiful haunting
blues that immediately riveted the entire juke. The soft
babble of noise grew into silence, and Bodeen nodded
his approval, backing him up with soft chords. The real
thing. A damn good blues. Much too soon it was over
and Jake nodded his satisfaction, let his guitar hang from
his neckstrap and folded his hands over the top of wood
polished slick with years of his sweat. Then he closed
his eyes and he waited his due. The milling crowd was
still yelling approval of his offering when the crooked
old man reached out and took his soul. The empty shell
collapsed and the crooked old man turned to leave. He
stumbled, weakened. It is harder sometimes for Death
to take an artist; they are curiously and passionately
connected to life and leave it with reluctant grace.

Inspired by Jake's solo, Bodeen started putting that
piano of his through its paces. When Jake didn't throw
down with him, Bodeen looked at him curiously.

"Hey Jake," Bodeen yelled at him, "you through already? The night still young youngster. Ain't you got no
stamina?"

Jake don't move, Jake don't answer.

Bodeen's chords dribble into silence and he looks
Jake over a little more closely. A couple other folk noticed that Jake was sitting kinda still. Gradually the noise
died down and a loud blaring silence filled the juke.

He stared at Jake for a perplexed moment as if he didn't understand, or just didn't want to.

"Aw Jake," said Bodeen with a wry little shrug of a smile much like the one Jake had used on the crooked old man. "You had some good blues left in you boy."

And then, as if of their own volition, his hands began to play, a blues for Jake. A down-home delta midnight blues. A riff on Jake's last melody. Folks that was there that night say to this day that Luke Bodeen had never before played a blues so mean. They heard that moist delta wind in every note, felt that lucky old morning sun lazy rippling on the river and those long late jukejoint nights wringing every drop of pleasure out of a hard delta life. Luke Bodeen played the blues and folks felt lowdown horizons and long backbreaking cotton days easing up off their souls. One day we all get to rest. One day we all get to lay our burdens down. Till then Luke Bodeen gon play the blues.

Oh Lord I love this delta
I love this delta so
Its been a long hard life Lord
But I sho do hate to go

O yes, Bodeen played a blue-black delta night velvet blues that morning, some Rest me Lord, rest me easy blues, I've traveled a long hard road and I'ma weary weary man. Boy played so good Dawn herself rose glowing in the East, came through the open front door of the juke and sat in a corner, patting her feet and nodding her head to some mighty fine blues.

Rest me Lord, rest me easy
I'm laying this burden down

Enough crying; the blues is for singing not crying. Bodeen drained a bottle and let his left hand go walking. They sent ole Jake out on the kind of rowdy defiant note befitting a good bluesman. By the time they were through with it, folks were hooting and fieldhollering and a good time was being had by all. And ole Jake, he just a sitting there. Folk claim he played on all night long. Say if you listen real good you can hear him to this day. A downhome delta bluesman on his last gig.

I'm laying this burden down

Barely breathing and as still as a mountain's heart, Melvira Dupree sat at her altar, eyes closed, hands resting in her lap, candles lit at the four corners of the earth. The sun was in the sky.

The door opened. She sighed, she smiled, she opened her eyes.

"Hey baby." He laid down on the pallet. Tough guy. Her eyes were indulgent and she snuggled up to him. Absently, his arms went around her and she was suddenly limp against him, laughing and crying and gasping for breath. She smelled liquor, but this once she didn't mind.

"O Lucas, I'm so sorry."

Bodeen half smiled, half frowned. A question. Maybe two.

"Jake," she explained, "I'm so sorry baby."

Though not half as sorry as she would have been had not her man come walking through that door this morning.

Bodeen shrugged and smiled crookedly. He so cool. She kept hugging him with a grateful sobbing passion that confused him. He resisted it, afraid to be touched by true emotion, but gradually letting himself unknot into the gently demanding warmth of a woman who cares.

When he spoke it was like he wasn't really speaking to her, or even himself, it was as though he was talking to God. "Just don't seem fair somehow. He woulda been a good bluesman. But he didn't get to do his best stuff. Just don't seem fair."

"Since when," Melvira murmured into his neck, "did bluesmen expect life to be fair?"

Bodeen looked at her a perplexed moment before suddenly unleashing a cathartic god-defiant laughter rippling with lifelust. She snuggled up on him, stroking him and giving him that special mellow treatment. Wasn't nothing for giving that old boy fortitude like Melvira beaming approval on him.

He snuggled deeper into her arms, warm and satisfied, feeling that tension just melt away, a king on a throne. "You feel like giving me some loving baby?"

Her voice is so soft he more feels it than hears it. "Been waiting with it for you."

Then she held him like he needed to be held, playing him like the fine old instrument he was.

———————

Back on the delta, long before books and poems, it was the blues that kept the record. The blues told the stories, they held the delta's history, they held the delta's soul. Bluesmen now, they come and go, but a good blues will last forever. What bothered Bodeen most was that Jake's stories had died untold.

I been born in real hard times
my road been long and hard

Bodeen perplexed the congregation at the juke over the next couple of weeks. He was spacey, very spacey, playing sparse and moody blues, doing more drinking than playing. Folks figured he was still in mourning for his partner and pretty much left him alone, but truth be known Luke Bodeen was way too much into himself to mourn anybody for long. What concerned Bodeen was how all this affected Bodeen. He figured if a good bluesman as young as Jake could just up and die like that, that meant that he could die too. Now, strange as it may sound to you, this was news to Lucas Bodeen. Made him real aware of the fact that he was damn near 40. Well —37. Close enough. He could suddenly feel every ache and pain. The bad shoulder. The stiffening hands. The funny little constant pain under his left rib.

He had learned to live with them. What can you do? You reach a certain age and every year something else quit functioning properly. He hit a discordant minor chord and reluctantly looked back on his life. He's lived fast and hard, Lucas Bodeen has, using up his years without a thought to tomorrow. Without realizing it, he started exercising his hand. What would he be when he couldn't be a bluesman? He looked up over the top of his piano at the crowd of blackfolk having a goodtime on him. Enjoying life. Hard as it is. Bodeen couldn't help but smile. Blackfolks and the blues. Finessing the hard-times and celebrating the goodones. Extracting strength from adversity. His eyes misted. It made him feel good to do for blackfolks. To be able to.

He let his piano stretch out some. Folk heard him getting into it and fingers start popping, bodies start swaying, folk start smiling. Lucas Bodeen never thought too much about stuff like this before. Life. Death. Purpose. Been too busy living life to much think about it. But there come a time in a man's life when he come to wonder if he been wasting his allotted time on the planet. Bodeen had always just kinda assumed that a serious bluesman would be left alone long enough to do his thing. Up to now the blues had took every kind of hammer life ever threw at him and defeated em. Tribulations that crushed other folk and sent em crying to God wasn't nothing but material for another blues for Luke Bodeen. But even the blues cant take on death and win.

Or can they?

They had a Victrola down at the Sweetwater General Store. Would play it for the folks who sat on the porch discussing the news of the day. When Bodeen took to coming by the Sweetwater General Store most every day just to play that Victrola, he became a prime topic of conversation. "You know, the bluesman that stay over

down at the Creek with the conjure woman," didn't listen to but one record, Mamie Smith's new blues record.
First one ever recorded. One of those new race records
by Okeh. He'd wind it up, play it, wind it up, play it again.
Good as it was, folk was tired of hearing it by the time
he quit coming round. But he provided for hours of stim-
ulating conversation. Bluessingers bout as interesting
as conjurors.

Lucas and Melvira spent a lot of time sitting on the porch
of the cabin by the creek, Melvira in the porch swing,
Bodeen on the top step. Both of them liked that quiet
time together. The stars were bright and the moon was
a sharp crescent, the crickets were doing street-corner
harmony and the wind hummed in the trees. But tonight
Bodeen was drinking shine. He had been drinking all
night and Melvira wasn't happy. She was pushing that
swing in a hard steady rhythm. She didn't like his tendency to the high; it left his soul hazy. So often she was
with him in body only. He expected the complaint long
before it came.

"Bodeen," she said finally, from far away, "you been
high since I've known you. I really don't know who you
are. I wonder sometimes if you do."

He shrugged it off, they'd gone through this before.

Bodeen frowned in the dark. He wasn't used to nobody telling him what he could and could not do. "Look,
don't worry about what I do. I'ma grown man and when
I need a wife I'll tell you, okay. I was a drinking man
when you met me, okay."

"The gods . . ." she began angrily.

"What the gods got to do with this?" he interrupted, "the gods ain't got nothing to do with it. God is for folk that cant deal with real. I'ma bluesman. God don't have to carry my load."

She had nothing more to say. The angry squeal of the swing filled the night's silence. Bodeen fidgeted.

Off in the distance they heard a train blow. As always he lifted his head to listen wistfully. The call of a free man. The lines around her lips deepened. He didn't have to see them to know they were there.

"Working on a new blues," he said. An explanation. An appeal.

"Won't find it there."

He looked inside the jug, blew a jugband tune on it and laughed. "Maybe, maybe not."

Bodeen been drinking since he learned how to play. A couple of drinks to loosen him up and he'd let it all hang out, he'd take it to the wall. He had come to think of it as part of his tools. A piano, a sitting stool and a glass of brown Tennessee sipping whiskey.

He felt a little guilt because he knew she was right, but what could he do? He played a better blues when he was high, and as far as he was concerned that was the end of the argument. He'd tried to explain to her that he doesn't question what helps him play his blues and he resented her doing it. He took a long defiant swig from the jug to make his point. But he wasn't comfortable; he stood and began to pace the porch. Behind the facade of defiance, he's vulnerable to good folk looking down on him because he was a bluesman. A hard-drinking, hard-living delta bluesman. Felt folk didn't take him seriously cause he worked for himself instead of the man, cause he didn't plow the man's fields or work in his sawmill. Cause he didn't get paid for everything he did. Well, if nobody else, including his woman, took him seriously, he did. He was an artist by God, and a damn good one, and he'd clutch at any crutch that helped him be one. Don't care what it cost. Anybody could plow cotton, but a good blues was one of a kind. Wouldn't have existed except that he, Lucas Bodeen Jr., gave his heart to it. Worked at it harder than any cottonpicker he ever knowed. And one day they would respect him for it. Flaws and all. He tossed the sloshing jug into the darkness beyond the porch. And when he spoke his voice was serene with the kind of confidence that you got to be born with. "One day I'm gon do me a immortal blues Melvira. A blues that will still be here touching folk long after I'm dead and gone. A Luke Bodeen was here and he played a helluva blues blues. You can put that on my stone."

She couldn't help but feel him. His unquenchable belief in himself. His rampant manhood. Not only did she feel him, he moved her. Resonated deep within her. Her bluesman, her good-for-nothing-but-the-blues bluesman. One of the few things in this world that made her really feel, be really alive. Woman like Dupree need a man like Bodeen. Strong woman like that don't come alive unless she got a man of her own caliber to grow against. She knew there were problems ahead, but she refused to look too far. Or too close. Her own desires, her wants, her needs, would betray her power. She has been alone so long. They both realized how close they had come to losing something good and precious that night and when they went to bed they held on to each other long after the loving was done.

Got so that old rooster crowed any time of day. The daily gathering on the porch of the Sweetwater General Store speculated endlessly on it. Naturally those who had no idea spoke loudest and those that knew had nothing to say.

> *Legba. O Legba. Show me the way.*
> *Legba. O Legba. Open the door.*

Again Melvira Dupree sat motionlessly in her cane-backed rocking chair. Again the way was clouded, the door closed. Again her traveling spirit returned without knowledge. What then does she want of me? Melvira rose from her meditations with a muttered curse. The signs were mute and the gods would not deliver. To question is to expose yourself. To let others see a need is a weakness. Mystery increases her power and she is comfortable behind the mask—the conjure woman from down by the Creek who knows all things. But now she would have to show herself human afterall, to ask, to beg, who is my mother, why did she leave me, I need to know.

It quickly became clear to her that the elders of Sweetwater Arkansas were reluctant to talk about Effie Dupree. They mumbled, they shrugged, they told tales more myth than memory of a dark, big-boned woman who appeared in Sweetwater one drizzly day with a swollen belly riding high and claiming that the water of Sweetwater Creek was good for growing things. For seeds and beginnings.

Most of what little information Melvira was told about Effie Dupree she ignored as useless:

"When she left her, she left here flying, growed wings out her back just like that, going back to Africa I heard . . ."

"She could make your heart skip a beat, just by looking at you . . ."

"Draw snakes out of your belly . . ."

"She loved a carrion bird I once heard, had a demon spawn by it too . . ."

"Caused the river to run backwards once and . . ."

"Cure whatever ailed you . . ."

Now Dupree knew what hoodoo can and cannot do. What little she got that she could use was just enough to make her curious.

"Yo momma? Effie Dupree? I do recall she had two eyes when she came here," said Grandma Baxter. "Didn't stay much longer than it took to birth you, then she was gone. Pretty sure she had two eyes when she got here and not but one when she left. Couldn't swear to it though."

When Melvira left her yard, Grandma Baxter spit into the dust where she had stood and made the sign of the cross at her back.

"Effie Dupree," said one frizzybearded elder, "was that her name, I recollect her now, impressive woman, pretty gal, you look some like her. Strange for a conjure though, she didn't do much Works that I can recollect, just enough to get folks to leave her alone. Single-minded woman too I recall, like she had something to do and Lord help anybody that got in her way. Yep, she was strange enough, even for a hoodoo she was strange . . ." The old man looked over his shoulder, as if suddenly afraid that she would be there listening, "Yessir, even for a hoodoo she was strange. Onliest conjure I ever knowed of to pack a pistol."

The more she found out about Effie Dupree the less she knew. But even shadows tell tales—this much was clear—a strange (even for a conjure) driven woman who didn't think twice about sacrificing her own child and possibly her right eye for some hoodoo agenda. And now she wanted Melvira to come to her. The nerve. When Melvira Dupree went back to Hoodoo Maggie, she was calm, the signs were good, the decision was made. She would go, if only to spit in the woman's one eye.

"Where is she? My mother."

Shango curled into a furry ball on her lap, purring when she absently rubbed his twitching golden ears. Hoodoo Maggie pounded mortar with pestle, a monotonous, hypnotic sound. The powdered herbs inside misted the air around the two women.

"You going?" asked the old woman.

"I'm going."

The pounding mortar stopped. Maggie trained the twin pistols of her eyes on Melvira.

"You ready?"

She hesitated. All her life Melvira had been satisfied being Sweetwater's resident hoodoo. She could have easily spent her life here, nurturing her flock, confident in her power, never really challenged.

"Do I have a choice?"

The old woman worked the pestle in the mortar.

"Memphis."

"Memphis?"

"When she left here, she went to Memphis. Beale Street would probably be a good place to look for her."

Melvira frowned. Prickly and suspicious by nature, Melvira looked at the old woman with cautious, slitted eyes.

"I ain't against you child." Maggie spit a stream of tobacco into the soggy boot at her feet. "I'm the best friend you got."

Maggie passed her the fat redflanneled bag. "You come home to have your firstborn you hear, the water here is good for growing things."

The cat in Melvira's lap batted at the bag as it passed between them. Melvira hesitated before leaning over and kissing the old woman's forehead. They savored the moment and Melvira rose to leave. Behind her the steady sound of Hoodoo Maggie's mortar began again.

Oshun does he love me?
Oshun will he stay?
Oshun does he love me?
Oshun will he stay?

Bodeen slept.

Melvira's soft chant filled the room. She stirred a

steaming pot of chicken soup, dropping in onions and peppers, liberally spicing it up just like he liked it and trying to convince herself that what she was doing was right. She didn't mind doing it for other folks; why such trouble doing it for herself? She tasted a spoonful. Good, it was ready. From the folds of her dress she took a small stoppered jar of thick dark red liquid. She poured it into the pot but the power wasn't there, her heart wasn't in it. The only bond she wanted to use on her man was a far older magic. She took the pot to the door and poured it out. If he left, he left.

Oshun make him love me.
Oshun make him stay.

Melvira watched her man in his sleep.

As if sensing her appraisal, Bodeen's eyes suddenly opened and he stared up at her.

"You bout ready to move on Bodeen?"

Her voice was softer than the night, but the question snapped him fully awake from a halfsleep sluggishness. Sounded like the kind of question a man shouldn't half answer.

"Move on?" he asked.

That's not what she had meant to ask him. The words had just jumped willfully from her mouth, but now she wanted to know what he would say. And then again, she didn't.

"I'm going to Memphis," she said. "You coming?"

He frowned at the challenge he heard in her voice. Don't start up on me woman.

She knew she was pushing him, but she was already

angry. He would go, she knew, not necessarily because he wanted to be with her but because it was convenient for him. Like she was.

Bodeen raised himself up on his elbows so as to be on a level with her. She hadn't moved since she first spoke. The night was dark and quiet and in the east there was the faint hint of dawn in the sky. He could see her clearly.

"Why Memphis?"

She hesitated before answering.

"Effie Dupree," she said.

He almost laughed, but caught himself in time. Started to ask what and why, but he knew the answer. Dreams. Signs. Whatever. He tried to keep his voice neutral. His own folk were just a little ways down the river and he hadn't been home in three years. Guilt made him sneer.

"You're going to Memphis looking for a woman you haven't seen or heard from in almost thirty years?"

"Why do you care Lucas, you ready to go aren't you? So its a easy choice. What's it going to be, Memphis with me or Memphis without me?"

Bodeen didn't like being pushed. Even to do something he wanted to do. And wasn't accustomed to traveling with a band either. He was a solo act. Liked it best when he didn't have to account to nobody for nothing nor pay attention to nobody's druthers but his own. Lord knows he had been thinking of moving on. This was probably his best chance to break away clean. One thing leaving her in her own little town, entirely another taking her to Memphis where she didn't know anybody. He idly stroked her hip as he thought, fully aware of quality of the woman laying beside him. He had got kinda used to her being around, comfortable except for her efforts to civilize him and you gon run up on that with any woman. He had figured to keep her in play anyway, one of the many women that he had scattered throughout the delta. And he could always move on later.

She didn't move away; her eyes almost lit the darkness with their intensity. He shifted uncomfortably and looked away; sometimes it was like she could see straight through him. He knew that she wouldn't press it, she had gone as far as she ever would. It was on him, yes or no. She was already mad at him, he had taken too long thinking about it as it was. He was losing unnecessary points; he knew he was gonna go for it. The more he thought about it, the better it sounded. They could have a lot of fun in Memphis. And ain't nothing like having a good-looking woman on your arm for pulling other good-looking women.

"With." He laughed as he pulled her to him. "Okay?"

She didn't answer, still looking at him with those searchlight eyes. He pulled her closer, nuzzling her and gradually overcoming her resistance until they were snuggled face to face. He saw in her eyes a distance from which she watched him warily, but he was feeling so good he refused to accept it. Full of himself and knowing that she wanted to believe, he kissed her passionately, his entire body and being demanding a response she slowly gave. And gave. And gave. And just as he slid himself smoothly into her open invitation he heard himself murmur as if he meant it, "I ain't gon never give you up baby. Never."

· 2 ·

If

Beale

Street

Could

Talk

Like all the really good things in life, Melvira Dupree and Lucas Bodeen finally made it to Beale Street. They crossed over the bridge by wagon one bright Saturday morning. Once across the river Melvira was faced with the stolid brick squares of Memphis' budding eight-story skyline. On the otherside of the river, Arkansas dressed the delta horizon in the

bright shades of autumn and Melvira Dupree knew she
was leaving something behind. They caught a trolley up
Main to Beale. Melvira was fascinated. Memphis. She
may be leaving something behind but she knows already
that mysteries await her here, buried somewhere under
all the unfamiliar cars and big brick buildings right up
on each other. Trolley cars, hordes of people, every sin-
gle one of them in a hurry. They got off the trolley at
Beale and walked; Bodeen wanted to walk. "This is it,"
he told her with grinning excitement, "Beale Street."

Beale Street. About a mile of street running from the
riverbank deep into the heart of Memphis. From the
levee to Front Street was strictly rivertown, a wild and
wooly section crowded with rooming houses and hog-
nosed cafés for burly roustabouts and rivermen. Front
Street was strictly cotton. Baled on the sidewalk,
weighed in the storefronts, sold at the cotton marts. Between Front and Second you got your pawnshops and
your dry goods stores. Already the countryfolk were
coming in from the fields and farms of Tennessee, Mississippi and Arkansas, parking their horses, wagons and
Fords in the old Wagon Yard over on Second and Beale,
hunting down overalls, boots, dresses, plows and harness and the cherished gifts of unnecessary lace, hand
mirrors or red suspenders from Schwabs. Melvira was
fascinated, a hick from the sticks, mouth open and big-
eyed. Wow, look at all the people. Bodeen laughed at
her. "Girl you as bad as all the rest of these country
Negroes. Be cool, you with Lucas Bodeen now."

They turned down Hernando, a little side street off
Beale, and knocked on the door of a large white two-

story building with a line of steps leading up the side to a second-story balcony.

A big pretty solid woman in a long print dress came to the door.

"Lord help us all," she murmured with a pretty smile, "Lucas Bodeen is back in town." Her unruly laughter seemed to shake both her and the house. She and Bodeen hugged and danced into the street. They danced around pedestrians, totally unconcerned with the spectacle, so obviously pleased to see each other that Melvira couldn't help a twinge of jealousy at the obviously old and weathered intimacy between them. They finally ended up where they started, all tired and winded.

"Got a place for me Jackie J.?"

Jackie looked at Melvira and stepped back from Lucas.

"Rooms scarce Bodeen, so many folks coming through town these days. But you know Jackie J. gon always look out for you. You come on in here boy, who is this with you, she yours? You with this man honey? He a good ole boy, but he need domestication bad."

Jackie looked Melvira over with a curious eye and nodded sagely. "I spec you just might be the one to tame him though."

Glancing occasionally at Melvira, she led them up the steps to the second floor and gave Bodeen the key. "Pay me every week on Sunday. None of your stuff now Bodeen. You pays me this time." She slapped Bodeen's butt and he growled playfully, "Watch it now Jackie, you know I got a low threshold."

"You watch him good now girl," Jackie said affectionately as she left them. "The gals in this town just loves theyself some SweetLuke Bodeen."

Nice little place, big and airy. Facing Hernando. Two big windows and a little wood framed balcony. Lace curtains and a four-poster bed on the far wall. By the window, a chair for sitting, a small round table with a pitcher and a large bowl on it. Jackie always made sure he had a place to lay his head. They went back all the way. But this was nicer than usual, probably Melvira's doing.

Being that it was Saturday evening, Bodeen wanted to drop off their bags and go right out, but Melvira made him help her clean up the place first. Make it livable, make it theirs. By the time they got the place to Melvira's satisfaction it was dark out, but Saturday night found them strolling the street with all Beale Street's other stalkers of the night. Mostly working folk out for a good time, gardeners and maids, clerks and countryfolk in big grins and loud finery. But it was the fast-life crowd that ruled at night; the Beale Streeters were out in force. Predators. The gamblers and rounders, the easy riders and their fast-life women, all strolling to and fro amongst the dives and dance hall palaces. And music. Music coming from everywhere. From every joint and on every corner they was doing the blues. It was like the blues were a part of the air she breathed.

My boy Bodeen was in pig heaven, home sweet Beale Street. Noplace in the world I'd rather be.

"Over there," he said proudly, "is PeeWees. Professor Handy wrote the *Beale Street Blues* there. And over there is the Hole-in-the-Wall. And over there is the Monarch,

see, the big one there. They call it the Castle of Missing
Men cause there's a funeral parlor right behind it and
when folks get killed they just get drug out back for the
undertaker to pick up in the morning."

"You telling me truth Bodeen?"

"Truth?" He laughed, one of his best. "Who cares if
its true or not, it sounds good don't it?"

On every corner they stop and listen to the street
musicians, Bodeen running down pedigree. A jug band
played at the edge of Church's Park.

"Chatmon boys from down Bolton way, whole family
of them, they do good blues."

On Beale and Fourth there was a blind harp player,
with black shades and a weaving head. Played a mean
harp, but he didn't have but one line that he sang over
and over:

Every good man need a real good woman
Every good woman need a real good man.

"Gabriel," said Bodeen with a smile. "Best harp in
the city, but long as I knowed him he ain't played but
that one line."

As they walked through the streets, weaving amongst
the crowded press of folks, Melvira felt herself getting
caught up in the excitement, a taste of what Bodeen felt
about this Beale Street of his. Life in abundance. She
hadn't really wanted to come, but now that she was out
here they had a real good Beale Street of a time, going
from spot to spot, dancing, listening to the blues and
meeting Bodeen's old friends. Mostly women. They were
in the Monarch: a fancy place, she had never conceived

of anything remotely like it, cushioned seats built into the mirrored wall and a brass-railed mahogany bar, and people, people, people, when a pretty babybrown woman in a red sequined dress suddenly appeared out of the press of folks around them.

"SweetLuke Bodeen, I didn't know you were back in town."

The woman draped herself all over him.

"Hey Mamie, long time no see," he said absently. A piano player had caught his interest. A little wasted-looking guy with a New Orleans quiff haircut. Eyes squinted up from the smoke of a cigarette in the side of his mouth. Playing jazz off a score in front of him. It was the score that had Bodeen's attention.

"You the one been gone, I ain't heard from you since the last time you were in Memphis."

She glanced at Melvira and they spoke in the secret language of women. Mine, said Dupree. Mamie smiled lazily and undraped herself from Bodeen. Patted him on his cheek and moved on.

"See you around Bodeen."

"Who is that, SweetLuke?" asked Melvira.

"I don't know," he said, "but they call that music he playing Jass down in New Orleans. Ain't nothing but some warmed-over blues, I don't think much gon come out of it myself."

Lies and propaganda. He had played a little of that Jazz himself during one of his early New Orleans so-journs. Played with boys like mad Buddy Bolden and smooth Jelly Roll Morton and wasn't half as contemp-tuous as he sounded. Those New Orleans boys did some good work. Trained musicians a lot of them. He had been there when they started it. Had sneered cause it wasn't the blues; he liked the power of the word with his music. Bodeen remembered back when there wasn't no such thing as the blues, or jazz. He was a young boy then, about 15, maybe 16, new to Memphis, living off his wits and fascinated with the piano. They were playing ragtime back then. He'd haunt the places that they were playing it and watch the old guys' fingering. Then he'd go try to play the same thing on a log or a fence railing. There was this little place off Fourth where they had a player piano. Put a nickel in and pump away at the pedals. Follow the fingering. He put in many a nickel. Got so he could make a tune on a real piano and played whenever he could, more heart than skill. First they didn't even have to pay him, just let him play. Had all kinds of makework jobs, but nothing serious. Rather starve than do something other than learn how to play the piano better every day. Quit a good job in a minute to go make 15 cents a night playing piano.

Soon as he was good enough to get by, he went out on the road. Played jukes and pineywoods logging camps, anywhere he could, but his first real gig and true love was playing the riverboats. Stayed with the *Stacker Lee* for almost a year, big pretty double-decker steamboat, prettiest thing on the river. Boy loved getting paid to travel up and down the river playing piano. Thats when he picked up his love for Stetsons, brocaded vests and blouse-sleeved shirts. And a new sound. It was traveling up and down the river that he began to notice this new thing coming out of the roustabouts and the rivermen, started hearing it on the levees and in the logging camps and fields. He saw the way it was moving folk, and thats what he liked to do, move folk with his music.

They wasn't calling it the blues then, wasn't no such thing then as the blues. They were calling it cottonfield music and rivermusic, backcountry music, and one day down Tutwiler way he heard it called the blues, and he knew thats what he wanted to do, the blues, and thats what he wanted to be, a bluesman. By the time he got back to Memphis thats what he was calling himself, bluesman.

About 1906, 1907 maybe, he was playing piano over to PeeWees one night and he was doing his regular ragtime and the kind of partymusic that folks was accustomed to, but late that night he commence to playing some blues for them. Most of them didn't know where he was coming from and half of them didn't care. He got more perplexed frowns than he got approval. It's always rough on the cutting edge. They pretty much booed him off the stage that first night, hurt his feelings bad, liketa made him cry. Got into a big argument with some fool, made him so mad he almost pulled his pistol and killed somebody. But he came back the second night to do it again, and there was folks there who had come back to hear him do it again. And there were some who had heard Luke Bodeen was playing some of those blues they had been hearing about. They were a lot nicer to him that night. Ole PeeWee Virgilio, a stroking that handlebar mustache of his like he did whenever he saw a chance to profit, asked him what was it? "The blues," and where did he learn to play it? "the river." Asked him to come on back and play some more of it.

For a long while wasn't but him and about four or five other guys that could play that music. But by and by more and more folks come to ask for it, by name now, "Play the blues for me pianoman." Before you knew it every guitar and piano player on Beale was playing the blues, some of them better than him. Then Professor Handy put em on paper and the blues were born.

Put em on paper.

Now they had been playing em all along, but it wasn't till it was put down on paper that it became real for a lot of folk. Bodeen watched the jazz fella playing off the sheetmusic and thought about it some. Back when he started hardly anybody could read music. Bodeen played by ear, could play anything he heard once. But he couldn't read a lick. He had been playing a long time not to know how to read music. Blues have gone through a lot of changes since he started. Couldn't get by these days playing what he used to play back when he started, or even what he was playing the last time he was in town. A man had to keep up or fall behind.

"Excuse me baby," he said, rising up from the table, "be right back."

He went to the piano and watched the little guy play. Eyebrows lined, he tried to match the fingering with the sheetmusic. Melvira knew something was bothering him and watched him closely until he got involved in a poker game and she could focus on all the activity around her. So much going on. People all around her, ain't nothing in the world more interesting to a hoodoo than people. Memphis was going to be real enlightening. All this time she thought that she was knowledgeable sitting out there in the middle of nowhere. And this was just part of the world. It was humbling, how much she didn't know, how far she had to go. Her eyes were systematically sweeping the place, intently filing patterns and process, when Bodeen broke the bank. In the old days a gambling man that broke the bank was expected to set up the house till his winnings run out, or at least (lets be real here) till his extra winnings run out.

It was in the backroom of the Monarch that Bodeen did the trick, and before Melvira knew it she was on her first gravy train, grabbing Bodeen around his hips, her own grabbed by some big rascal behind her. Bodeen lead the delta snake-dancing line around the front room and on out into the street. First stop Hammitt's place. They set up the house, picked up some new believers, snake-danced through and on to the next place, picking up more folks at every spot. Had a real good time. Melvira laughed so hard her stomach was hurting and her mouth was tired. At one point Bodeen was so full of the feeling that he stopped and turned in the middle of the street. Melvira snake-danced right on into him and the rest of the line collapsed on itself, folks falling all over each other. Bodeen pulled her close and kissed her soundly while the rest of the gravy train cheered such a rousing display of spontaneous passion. O yes o yes, a good time was had by all.

Melvira Dupree let her hair down that night and it was sweated all down her back when Sunday's dawn found them flopping onto the bed still dressed and totally exhausted. Outside, Beale Street, so busy and alive that night, was now quiet and still, the air a Sunday morning crisp. They heard some muted morning sounds. Trolleys rolling through the streets. The bells of the many churches of Beale calling out the faithful. Somewhere close they heard Gabriel's harp. Mellow morning music now but the same old lyrics,

Every good man need a real good woman
Every good woman need a real good man.

Melvira laid her head on Bodeen's chest, exhausted, sated. A thick tendril of her loose hair tickled his nose and he stroked it out of the way with an affectionate hand.

"Enjoy yourself?" Bodeen asked her, half asleep, still stroking her hair.

"Not half as much as you did."

He snuggled into the warmth. Glad she was there. The sheet was fresh and clean, the room nice and homey. A woman's touch. Fell asleep without realizing it until the bed suddenly sprang and he popped his eyes open. Arms braced to either side of him, Melvira was looking down on him, thick mane of hair brushed back and tamed under a floppy hat. She was washed and dressed in her Sunday best and he raised a questioning eyebrow.

"Church," she said.

Melvira had been a regular churchgoing woman back in Sweetwater. Bodeen didn't understand why a hoodoo went to church in the first place.

"Church? What kinda hoodoo are you anyway?"

"Many roads to God Lucas Bodeen."

"What?"

"It feels good. You coming?"

He shook his head and settled deeper into the bed. Far as Luke Bodeen was concerned he had just got back from Church.

In 1919 Beale Street was still Beale Street, in spite of periodic *Cleanup Beale* campaigns. The first one was right after the election of Boss Crump in 1909. Prohibition had been decreed in Tennessee, but Crump didn't hardly enforce it; claimed it would cause more trouble than it was worth. Not to mention interfere with his colored votes. Boss Crump was ousted the first time by reformers in 1916 and they immediately called themselves cleaning up Beale. Beale survived. Another cleanup movement in 1919 by the Citizens Movement and Mayor Paine slowed it up some but not measurably so. Federal Prohibition had been passed in 1917 but not enacted yet.

So, in 1919, Beale was still Beale. But it wasn't just the honkytonk strip between Fourth and Hernando. By 1919 Beale Street was a community. There were quite a few colored Memphis communities growing from the steady stream coming in from the delta during the Great Migration, springing up wherever they could find land nobody else wanted, marginal land like over in the bayou and down along the levee with the river for back yard, but these hardy little communities took root and thrived. Places like Douglas and Orange Mound and Beale Street. Beale Street was the heart of colored Memphis. The majority of Beale Street folk never set foot in a juke or a honkytonk or a fancy joint in their lives.

Colored families shopped, paid bills, visited doctor and dentist, ate, got their hair done and went to church. As many churches as there were gin joints. This was Melvira's world. Now ole Bodeen, he never left the Beale Strip. Thats where the blues where and the congregations that appreciated them. But Melvira was fascinated with the new colored communities. Melvira had business to take care of.

East of the enormous mansions at the head of Beale, in gloomy swamplike areas, the Memphis hoodoos practiced their trade and did the Work. Crosses, curses, tricks, blessings, mojos and hands. Herbs for whatever ailed you and magic for what the herbs don't do. Melvira was fascinated. A hoodoo community. Back in Sweetwater she and Hoodoo Maggie had been the only practicing hoodoos. There were dozens in Memphis, hundreds, Memphis has always been a hoodoo town. Intimidated by the sheer number of them, Melvira was hesitant to declare herself a contender. It didn't take long, though, for her to realize that most of them were charlatans, fools preying on fools. Telling futures, raising haints, putting on and taking off tricks, selling potash and iodine for rheumatism, glycerine and calamine for complexion, peddling cut-rate dreams. A couple had some small power, fitfully understood, fitfully used, and of course, there were a few that knew what they were doing. And one or two who had true power. Knowledge of the way of things.

She asked up and down Beale. Neither hoodoo nor civilian knew anything of a one-eyed conjure. By her third week the question was rote, the answer expected.

"I'm looking for a one-eyed conjure woman nama Effie Dupree."

The old scraggly haired woman standing beside the hoodoo stand on Beale and Third was just a salesman. She spit on the ground and stirred the goods on the tray beside her; redflannel mojo hands, highjohnny conqueroos, fragrant bags of herbs and such in little paper sacks.

The little woman shook her head. "Never heard of her. Lemme sell you something dearie, some sacred sand, some good luck powder or some boss fix oil."

"Looking for Effie Dupree, a hoodoo woman. One eye."

"Don't know of no Effie Dupree. But I got a hand here that will help you find whatever is lost. Anything this Effie Dupree can do, I can do better."

When Melvira frowned at her she brushed her scraggly gray hairs back and looked at her closer.

"The Hootowl might know. According to him what he don't know ain't worth knowing." The old woman turned back to her table, "Want any more than that its gon cost you."

"Where can I find this Hootowl."

"Pressing it ain't you?" She looked again at Melvira Dupree and decided to answer. "He tie up a riverboat at the foot of Beale, you find him there."

Luke Bodeen was a known man on Beale and it didn't take him long to find a job playing piano down at the Hole-in-the-Wall. The Wall was a strange joint, brought in a stranger crowd. But it was a good blues crowd and he guessed that was what counted. The Hole-in-the-Wall was known as a hard place to play. They penalize you for everything, five cents for spitting on the dice, or the floor, five cents for missing the horn, five cents for breathing. Smart man didn't gamble down at the Hole-in-the-Wall. And what's more he came armed. When the house got nervous because they had too many badmen in there they'd call the law. The law would raid the joint and everybody would start throwing their pistols and knives on the floor. The house would come through scooping up all the weight laying on the floor and thereby keep the killing down. First night that Bodeen played there, around midnight or so, he was double rolling his bass when shots rang out and bullets suddenly splintered his piano right beside his fingers. "Critics," he muttered as he drew his hognose from inside his jacket and went over the back of the piano. Second week the owner, old Jim Kinane, came up to him while he was playing and said that he thought Bodeen needed to put a band together.

"Blues changing Bodeen," he said around his cigar. "You bout the only serious bluesman I know still playing solo."

Hard for a old dog like Bodeen to change, but you know how he feels about getting left behind. He pondered it some, not much. Then he went out and rounded up a couple of guys that he had known from back when and they put together a houseband for Kinane. Got Gabriel for his harp and Heavy and the Hat. Heavy was a big man with a deep scar ringing his neck, some say put there by the Hat. That old boy would just sit there, just a plucking at that bass guitar of his like nothing else in the world mattered. The Hat was tall and lean and always under a big white Stetson. Playing that guitar. Two guitars was guitar heavy, but those boys worked together. They argued all the time, but it made for some good blues.

They were all known bluesmen, didn't take them long to pull a regular crowd. Decided to call theyself the Sacred Blues Band. A big hassle. Gabriel drank too much and didn't none of them believe in rehearsals. When Bodeen did get them together and reasonably sober they had more fun than work. Not a one of them knew how to read music. Didn't bother the fellows, they all had ears and they never had any trouble making no blues, never had any trouble moving the congregation either. So he begged and pampered and babied and berated because when the Sacred Blues were on they were on, and when they were really down couldn't nobody on the planet do a better blues. Did a little some of everything at first, the Sacred Blues did, weddings, rallys, hoedowns, rent parties, you name it. Liked playing for whitefolks better than they did for their own. Whitefolk pay you five dollars a man, feed you and you outta there by 11:30, 12 o'clock. Blackfolk? Two dollars a man, you buy your own food and you ain't outta there till the rooster crow. The Hole got to be a steady gig, though, and they didn't have to hang around over at PeeWees with the rest of Beale's musicians waiting for somebody to hire you. Still he went there often just to hang out and cut head. PeeWees was the spot for cutting head and keeping your game tight.

It was nice being back on Beale. He could feel himself getting better every day, picking up new licks, stretching out, Beale did that to you, you either kept up or fell behind. Music was all around you and it was as important to other folks as it was to you. You constantly being exposed to new licks and you constantly growing. On Beale in those days you could live music. Melvira complained about the time he spent out. Sometimes dawn to dawn. She thought he was out there chasing the women. Seem like a hoodoo ought to know better. Ol' Bodeen, he was just chasing the blues. He should have explained it to her better. Melvira never did understand him and Beale, but he never gave her a chance to. Gets real testy when anybody dare question how he spends his time. Boy come in with the rising sun, sit down on the side of the bed and start taking off his shoes.

"Good morning," she murmurs. Two words so thick with irony they would have been better left unsaid.

"Morning."

A pause. Dawn breaks. She asks in spite of herself.

"Where you been Bodeen?"

"Nowhere."

Her passions cloud the way.

"Two days of nowhere?"

"Don't start up on me. Okay? I been out. Okay?"

Phwwwtt. She turned to the wall. Okay.

Big Jim Kinane telling him that he was out of step bothered him some. He didn't realize just how much until the day he walked into PeeWees and saw W. C. Handy sitting at a corner table by himself. It was early yet and

PeeWees wasn't really jumping, just a few folks scattered around the big front room, a couple of guys he knew getting their horns out of the back. He checked in at the cigar stand to see if he had any messages. None. What the hell, no harm in asking. He went to Handy's table with a bottle in his hand. Handy was known to be a drinking man.

"Mind if I sit down 'fessor Handy?"

"Not at all Bodeen." Handy held out his glass and Bodeen poured him a good one. They sat listening to the quiffheaded piano player.

"Bodeen," said Handy, rubbing his bald spot, "gave any thought to working with me, I can always use a good piano."

He had asked before and Bodeen laughed it off; Handy didn't really play his style. Bodeen considered himself a musician and could play most anything he heard. But what he liked was the blues.

"Come on now 'fessor Handy, imagine me in one of those uniforms you dress your boys in."

They laughed. Bodeen tended to Stetsons and vests and silk shirts with bright red sleeve garters. Dressed like the riverboat gambler he wished he was. Handy's boys dressed in red band uniforms with epaulets and plumed hats. In those days, Handy had two, three bands that he hired out as Handy bands. All of them stayed busy. Played a formal band-music style. Classically trained. He had told Bodeen once that he came to the blues when playing a gig down in Cleveland Mississippi one evening and he was asked to play some "native" music. When he couldn't deliver, the crowd asked if he would mind some locals sitting in. The locals got all down in the gutter. Down-home blues. Made more in tips thrown out than Handy was making for the night. Handy went right home and got to work. Wrote himself some blues. Wasn't much as blues go, but he was the first one to write em down and made the rep for it.

"Say man," said Bodeen, "uh, I'll play for you, wear one of your uniforms and everything, if you, uh teach me how to read music."

Handy looked him over, absently stroking his trumpet player's lip circle and trying to judge Bodeen's sincerity.

Bodeen was sincere all right. If other folk could play off sheetmusic, then he wanted to be able to do it too. He was leery of asking somebody to help him. Messed with his image. Delta Luke Bodeen. Bluesman extraordinaire.

"Well you know I don't really teach music Bodeen."

"Please man."

Handy shifted in his seat to look at Bodeen. "Why you want learn musicology Lucas, been doing fine enough without it all these years."

Bodeen thought about it some, not much, didn't have to. "I ain't keeping up man. I gotta keep up. Me and the blues both. Gotta stay ahead of the changes. Both of us."

Handy smiled and snorted reflectively. He took another drink and wiped down his thick germanic mustache. "Ever been," he said, "down to where the Southern cross the Dog?"

"Mississippi," said Bodeen, "down Tutwiler way. I been through there once or twice."

Handy nodded. "Thought so." He rubbed that bald-spot head of his. Took a drink. Religious man, dressed like a deacon in the church. Held himself so. He stood and went to the piano, came back with some sheetmusic. "Okay Bodeen, look, this top line there is the treble line, thats your right hand, bottom one is the bass."

Melvira shifted at her altar. A client downstairs. A very disturbed one. Waves of anxiety ripple the air. An older woman. Alabama woman. Standing in the street downstairs looking up at the balcony. Melvira stirred at her altar but she didn't rise. She had minutes more meditation before the woman downstairs would make her decision. Dupree had set up her consultation table in a corner and curtained it off with a patchwork quilt covered with the quilted circled X of the crossed sun. Business started slow but the word got around, a new hoodoo over on Hernando, she do good work. Downstairs, the woman from Alabama made her decision

The
Hoodoo
Sign

and started up the stairs, thick work boots clumping heavily on the weathered wood. A heavy woman, ponderous, stolid, a rock on known ground. Melvira stilled herself and touched the woman's burden. A man. Family. Melvira allowed herself a small quick smile. She would help the woman climbing her stairs. Who would help Melvira Dupree?

Back in Tupelo, Cato Robinson had been a good family man and even better farmer, justly proud of his ability to bring in a good crop no matter how bad or rocky the land. Give him good smooth bottomland and he could bring in seven, eight bales of cotton from a one-mule farm. And thats putting a little land aside for greens, onions, watermelon, turnips and tomatoes. Cato was a hard-working man, and his idea of fun was to spend Saturday evening on the Post Office porch swapping tales and commentary with the more regular town loafers. For 15 years he and Cora gave their lives to the delta. They had stood up to killer hurricanes from the Gulf and hooded riders of the Mississippi night. They were still there when the boll weevil come up out of Texas in 1913. Didn't nobody understand the weevil's ways back then, how they gon kill the cotton no matter what you do. They were with old Colonel Ragardie that year. The boweevil was bad enough, but the Colonel didn't ever give his tenants enough fertilizer, and without fertilizer you got poor cotton. Didn't do hardly three bales that year. Moved down to Jemsen's place and was allotted to rough rocky land that wouldn't hardly take a plow, broke three of those old wood beamed Dixie Boy plows in a month. Cato had to go into debt to get him one of those good iron beam Vulcans that could tote a big mule over heavy rocks without breaking. Only problem was that he signed a full note on it. Man cant read should never sign no banker's notes without first having it read to him square. They took everything he had that year. After he had paid them the cotton due his whitefolk took his mule, his wagon, his hogs and his new iron beam plow. Cleaned him out again in 1916. Found him some smooth easy land in 1917, good landlord, he was prepared to stay, cotton got sleeted out that year. Had to replow when the wet land hardened in around his roots and stunted his cotton. Didn't even get three bales that year. It do indeed seem all God's dangers ain't whitefolk. Took what he had to the mill and found out cotton had fell to a nickel a pound. Those were some rough years, '12 to about '17, but then none of them were easy. They had gotten married in '88, moved off his daddy's place in '92, had the four boys and five girls late. Kids couldn't get a decent education at the county schools for coloreds cause the schools got closed down and the kids pulled out whenever the county's farmers needed them for picking, plowing or planting. But they were good kids. They still had a chance and Cato was determined to give it to them. Cotton was selling good during the war years, they had that good smooth land and they had just about caught up to life when old man Robinson died and his son took over. Forced them to sign a note on their property, their crops and their household goods. Cato and Cora knew what was coming, they had been there before. Started listening wistfully to stories told of the Promised Land—Chicago. Plenty work to be had for all God's children in Chicago, said the *Chicago Defender*, store-bought clothes and inside toilets. A blackman could be a man in Chicago, he heard. Folks had been leaving for awhile now. Many of his neighbors were already gone. Every family had somebody gone north, some families left entire. And more leaving every day. He sat down and talked it over with Cora. The kids deserved better. But all they know was farming. They watched their whitefolks get more and more disturbed as longsuffering sharecroppers left plows standing in the fields and crops rotting in the ground. Laws were passed tying them to the land, more fatback was included in the rations, meetings were held telling them they didn't really want to go north, nobody there to take care of them, and its godawful cold, even if Sallymae's boy was sending her 30 a month from Detroit. Thirty dollars. Can you believe that? Boy came home driving his own automobile last year. Wearing a fancy suit too. He wasn't never that sharp a boy, imagine what a hard-working man could do. And then came the summer of 1917 and they lynched that labor recruiter from Chicago. Called him a agitator, said he was stirring up the nigras. Cato and Cora made the decision to go to Chicago then. Didn't get to leave till almost three years later, but the decision was made then. They went deep into debt that year and was still owing young Robinson when they finally packed all their belongings in that creaky old truck of theirs that wasn't no more going to make it to Chicago than the man in the moon. Placed Junior, Roscoe, Charlene, Marian, Coral, Dexter, Kathleen, Willy and Willie carefully in little cubbyholes made by their haphazardly stacked belongings, tied them down good so that they wouldn't fall off on the way, and joined one of history's great migrations. Set off for the Promised Land and got as far as Memphis. Decided to lay over a couple of weeks to get their bearings and assess the condition of that old truck before going on. Two months later they were still in Memphis, living in an apartment at 170 Beale, truck broke, money gone,

Cora taking in washing and Cato mesmerized by the perfumed and pampered women he found on Beale. Cora couldn't compete, all the soft roundness long since squeezed out of her by hardtimes on the delta. She tried most everything she knew to hold a man before setting off one noon in her best dress and her new hightop boots, asking a man on the corner of Beale and Hernando if he knew of a good hoodoo.

He pointed down the street, "Third house from the corner. I understand that she do good work. Second floor, walk up those steps and knock on the door."

Cora stood for long reflective moments at the bottom of the steps. Then she set her shoulders. She had survived everything the delta ever threw on her, she wouldn't let Beale Street beat her. Or her family.

When she walked in, Melvira motioned her to sit. "I can bring him home," she said, "it'll be up to you to keep him there."

Cora relaxed. Life might be worth living after all.

Other night Sacred Blues was taking a break and Lucas Bodeen was sitting at his piano down in the Hole-in-the-Wall. He was trying to play piano off this music he had written, but it didn't sound like it was supposed to. Wasn't hardly notes much less music, and he's trying so hard he's dripping sweat all over the piano keys. He worked on it for awhile, then, to relax himself and reassure anybody that needed reassuring, he closed his eyes and just let the music kinda flow through his fingers onto the keys. His basic lick, don't have to think about it or anything, just put his hands out and let em play. Sounded good too; sometimes its just there, you're hooked up and can do no wrong, you come up with sounds and chords you know you'll never hear again cause you playing what you feel. Folks started amening him, fingers started popping. Getting a little rhythm from the crowd caused him to stretch it out some and he was doing good blues when suddenly his treble keys sprung a shrill protest. He opened his eyes and saw a red silked hip sitting on his piano. Pissed him off at first, what the hell. But the more he followed the red silk curves of that hip, all in proper place and proportion, the more he's smiling, till by the time he got past those pretty brown shoulders and was looking Mamie in her pretty brown face, he was giving her his Bodeen best. She was looking down on him with that look she had that just dared a man to try something. Flaming Mamie, they called her. One of the finest women in Memphis. A big healthy gal. His nature stood up on its hindlegs and drooled. Mamie was one of his allotted women on the planet. There some women on the planet that just belong to him. He could tell the minute he meet one. Mine. Like the Lord made this one just for him. Melvira was one. So was Mamie. When he looked in her eyes they were all he could see, his whole world, he had to make an effort not to lose himself in them. She smiled. She knew she could play him.

"Lucas baby, I was wondering," she purred, "if you were in a mood to play something I like."

He ran riffs up the treble keys next to her hip, playing with himself and her too. "Just what is it that you like girl?"

"You know what I like Lucas," she said in a voice so steamy his toes curled. "Just play."

She slid off the piano, red dress pulling back over those long thick legs, poor piano keys again protesting with a sprung chord. Big hot brown eyes still holding his, that luscious body of hers began weaving to his music, responding to his every note like her body was the instrument being played. A primal courting thing, like they the only two folk in the place. He trebled with his right hand and those big titties of hers shifted around like heavy globes of water, the nipples hard hot points in his palm. He rumbled his left-hand base and her hips jerked, like his fingers in her instead of on the keys, faster, harder, daring him to follow. His nose flared and his manhood rose howling at the moon. His throat suddenly dry, he licked his lips, slowly, holding her eyes, her body writhing under his hands, her every move saying she was his for the taking, her passion his to command. She began singing, a purring song that only he heard. Spellbound, he picked up the pace, throwing lowdown chords at her thrusting hips harder and faster, driving her like he was . . . whoa, he thought, let me quit. He pulled his hands from the keyboard and wiped them on the starched khaki leg of his pants. He couldn't hang. This was one woman he couldn't play with.

He drew a deep breath. It helped some. "You gon get me in trouble," he said.

"I'ma get you into something," she laughed. A silver tinkle that ran across the back of his neck.

He started playing his piano again, a soft calming piece.

She puckered her big red lips at him. "Chicken," she said and walked away. It was all he could do to just sit there and watch her walk away, that slick red dress alive on a body just built for his hands. His lips. His tongue. His undivided attention. Boy you better quit. He forced himself back into his music. Trouble. The woman's name is Trouble.

Trouble O Trouble, stay away from me, Trouble O Trouble, let me be.

Hmmm. Put a little of that heat that he was feeling just then in there and he might have a decent blues in this. Burn off that energy and keep him out of Trouble. He put a little passionate rumbling bass chords on it and growled:

> *Trouble o Trouble, stay away from me*
> *Trouble o trouble wont let me be*
> *Look like I got trouble, sweet trouble,*
> *stalking me . . .*

"What happened?" asked Gabriel. He had missed the play, but he heard the music. Across the floor Mamie turned to look at him with a knowing smile. Little tease.

"Trouble," Bodeen said absently, mind half watching Mamie, half on the music he was making.

"Ain't like it ain't the kind of trouble a man can't handle," laughed Heavy.

"Bodeen a married man," said the Hat. "I like the song though. That Mamie a pistol ain't she? Melvira saw that one she'd hoodoo you for sure Bodeen."

They cracked up. They thought it was cute. Keeps you honest when your buddies like your woman. Sometimes he could do without prying eyes and loose jokes. Hard to be a good man in a world full of candy. Mouth still dry, he watched Mamie blend back into the crowd. Woman sure did know how to move. Some young fancyman whispered in her ear and drew a bubbling laugh from her. Pissed him off. Him and Mamie had a hot thing a couple of years back. God he'd like to get his hands on that again. Just once. She looked up and caught him looking, her tongue flicking out over her red red lips.

"Chicken."

Now its a well-known fact that a man making music speaks to women in a language they understand. Being a real-live delta bluesman, Luke Bodeen gets a lot of play. Occasionally he'd get a blank check: "Whatever you wanna do bluesman is okay with me." He liked that. He liked that a lot. Happened enough that he tended to consider the attention of women his due. He would tell you in a minute—Cant love all of you but I do like to play, I do like to be the center of female attention. For a fact I consider every piece I ever did to be a magical lovepoem and every woman thats ever been touched by my song is supposed to fall madly and forever in love with me.

Especially you.

Listen my friend, never mistake the tale for the teller or the teller for the tale. Of the two the tale is always the greater power.

———————

When he got home that night Melvira was still up and sitting at her altar. Bodeen was half pissed about having to pass up on Mamie. Muttering to himself about how nice it would be to be a free man again. Could be riding her now, big healthy body firmly in hand. Without realizing it he grunted at the thought. Melvira looked up at him. Like she knew what was on his mind. Man cant even think to himself. He knew she had waited up for him. Knew she wanted to talk.

"A woman came to see me today . . ."

"I'm kinda tired Melvira, maybe tomorrow."

He lay down in the bed, making it clear he was in no mood to listen. He rarely was, considered her problems self-made. This thing about her mother. About Memphis. Her flock. People hungry. People sad. Bodeen accused her of gratuitous agonizing. Said she went out of her way to have problems, said he had enough problems of his own without worrying about other folks problems. Disappointed, she turned back to her altar carrying the sudden realization that Bodeen didn't really need her. Didn't need anybody in his life.

One misty Sunday morning Melvira Dupree left the Beale Street Baptist Church and walked through the shadow of St. John the Baptist toward the river. She found the little flatbed houseboat tied up a little downriver, out of the way of the rivertraffic, a flat square of a boat with a squat box house sitting in the middle of it. She walked down the cobblestoned riverfront until she got to the weathergray boat swaying softly in the easy rivercurrent. The little house seemed warped in some way. As she got closer she saw that it was made of driftwood, so cunningly designed it seemed seamless, one big godcarved piece. The smell of old wet wood stung her nostrils and rivermist plastered hair and dress to her body in an oddly comforting embrace. It rocked gracefully when Melvira walked across the gangplank and pushed aside heavy curtains leading into a small square room. Candles tease the darkness. An altar built of a tree trunk was arrayed with offerings of food and flowers and carved figurines stained with candle drippings. An elder sat on a wide wooden stool in the middle of the small room, a wide man with a huge forehead bracketed with feathery tufts of white hair and a thick gray flecked beard sculpting his chin. Seven tribal scars were carved into each side of wide angular cheeks. She looked but couldn't see past the mask. He was like a great rock with most of it buried deeply into the ground. He was dressed in blue overalls; his chest was bare and covered with sparse gray hairs. He leaned back on the stool he was sitting on and hooked his thumbs in the straps of his overalls.

"What can I do for you mam?"

"I'm told you might be able to help me find someone."

"Its possible. I'm good at finding things. Who is it?"

"Effie Dupree. She's in the business."

"Indeed." He appeared unaffected but she sensed a difference in his attitude, "And tell me Miz, uh . . ."

"Dupree."

"Ah. Miz Dupree. Tell me, are you also, as you say, in the business?"

"I am."

"And this Effie Dupree. A relative of yourn?"

"My mother."

He pursed his lips and rubbed his jaw reflectively. The seven scars rearranged themselves on his cheek.

"Do you know her?" Melvira asked impatiently.

"Hard to know yourself, much less anybody else. I'd have to; no wait." he bowed his apologies to her evident irritation, "Forgive me. A straight question deserves a straight answer. No, I do not know of your Miss Effie Dupree."

"Then why the questions?"

"I'm just curious about anything having to do with hoodoo that go on in this town."

"So you cant help me."

"Well no Miz Dupree, I didn't say that. I will look into this and get back to you if my inquiries are fruitful."

Disappointed, she stood and started to leave, "You can get in touch with me at . . ."

"Oh I know where to get in touch with you Miz Dupree. Like I said, I do like to keep up with what goes on in this town. I'm told you do good work. Good. Always room for a good conjure in this town. This a conjure town."

Melvira nodded curtly. "Thank you for your time." She turned and pushed through the heavy curtains into the air. She crossed the gangplank and walked uneasily up the bluff. It was as if she felt the musty old rivercity watching her. Memphis Tennessee. Scared city of Ptah. He who thought the world, said it in a word and then it was so. A conjure town. Walk the streets. Ask the elders. Probe beneath the surface and there are secrets in Mem-

phis Tennessee that will change your life forever. Stay
long enough and you will understand the meaning of
holyground.

Bodeen was tomcat fidgety. For all practical purposes,
he was already gone, lost to Beale Street's blues, women
and fast life. Melvira more often than not didn't know
where he was spending his time. Deathly afraid of being
left alone again, she tried harder. The listening ear. The
warm comfortable body that fits like a old shoe. The
heart that understands when no one else does, or can,
that extra drop of butter that she knows he likes on his
yams. A companion. A friend. Woman and mate.

When that didn't work, she started bitching: his long
hours, his drinking, the cocaine he occasionally bought
down at Lehmens Drug Store in twenty-five-cent tins.
That demon, she called it, more mad at herself for showing that she cared than at him for being him. Got so that
she didn't hardly have to open her mouth before he
would turn his back, put his hat on and leave. Luke
Bodeen had a low tolerance for hassle. He would walk
down to the Hole-in-the-Wall, trying to remember what
it had been like being a free man. It was vague, like it
was some dream that you can only partly remember
come morning. He did remember when he could go
where he wanted when he wanted, spend his money
like he saw fit. Could leave town right now if he was of
a mind to. Could do what he damned well pleased.

He walked into the Hole-in-the-Wall still fuming,
swearing to himself that he was just waiting for the op-

portunity to walk without feeling guilty about it. Fat chance. Woman kept him feeling guilty.

"Hey man," laughed Heavy, "howcome you look so foul boy?"

"That woman of mine is dogging me."

He sat down at the piano and hit a rough chord, still muttering, mostly to himself, "I just don't see why I got to always feel guilty about being me. I'm the same me I always been, I don't hurt nobody. As long as I'm doing my blues cant nobody tell me nothing."

He's riffing chords while he's muttering, rough atonal blues, working off that bad energy.

But Bodeen ain't the kind of person to stay mad at anybody too long. When he got home that night he was in a pretty good mood. She hadn't waited up for him. Had quit that awhile back. He walked over to the bed and looked down at her tenderly. The moon coming in through the window threw her face into a soft light, and he stood there looking at her for a long moment. She was such a beautiful woman when she was asleep and all the rigid lines etched into the corners of her mouth softened. He felt a sudden welling of affection for her, wanted to take her in his arms, feel that little smile of hers that lit up his days and nights more than any sun or moon could do. Hear that murmuring little giggle that meant she was happy. His sweet strange stangaree baby. It was a magic moment, one of those special loving moments that make life worthwhile. He had had many with her. He started to wake her, tell her just how much he loved her, how much she meant to him, that he'd try to do better. He moved toward her and hesitated. She was probably still mad at him. When Bodeen got mad he wasn't mad but a minute; when Dupree got mad she stayed mad. Soon as he woke her those hard lines would grow in the corners of her mouth. While he stood there the moon passed behind a cloud and the room went dark. The moment was gone.

Bodeen come to spend more and more of his time down at the Hole-in-the-Wall. Melvira spent her days watching the steady stream of blackfolk coming in to Memphis from all around the delta. She listened to their call and brooded, and when Melvira brooded, the whole world knew of it. The Hootowl had sent for her a couple of times, summonses that she ignored. She no longer tried to share her concerns with Bodeen. There was very little they had to say to each other these days that wasn't a complaint or an argument, and neither of them were very surprised the night he left in a fine and righteous huff. Actually they had done well. Beale Street circa 1920 was breaking up colored families as quick as they came to town.

It had been an argument like many of the others they had been having lately, Melvira pissed and enumerating his many faults. He didn't even hear her words, just the shrill hammer of her voice.

"Bodeen, why do you always have to be high? I don't ever know where you are. You don't give anything to me." Blah blah blah.

Suddenly he'd had enough, and his open palm cut across his body in a abrupt dismissal.

"Hey forget this, I'm gone. I'm outta here."

He started throwing clothes into his traveling bag.

"Bodeen . . ."

Soft. A plea. Her greatest fear.

"Don't nothing I do please you woman, and I'm tired of feeling bad about being me."

"Bodeen . . ."

She couldn't bring herself to beg any further. She had known this day would come. First her mamma, now her man. A cold place in her heart that she had long prepared said Never Again. Both her face and her heart closed tight. Bodeen was too busy spewing righteous steam to notice.

"I need a break baby. I'm tired of you preaching at me, I'm tired of feeling bad about being me. I don't dog you. You act like I'm dogging you."

He realized that she had stopped calling his name and frowned, waiting for her abject apologies. He didn't really want to go.

"I been too easy for you haven't I?" she said emotionlessly, "I don't cost you anything, do I?"

No damn good. Woman obviously needed to be taught a lesson. He walked to the door and put his hand on the knob. He hesitated. Her one last chance to beg. Reassurance of his power over her. Beg me woman.

"If you leave, don't come back."

She knew when she said it how he would respond. He was a hardheaded man, her Bodeen, and would have to be shown.

The slam of the door shook the building.

The moment the door closed behind him Bodeen

wondered if he was making a big mistake. Boy wanted to turn around immediately. But if he went right back she would be in command. What kind of man would he be then? And then too a part of him felt a big relief. Hey he was a free man again, at least for a week or so. He could hoot and holler and have a good old time without feeling bad about it. Give him some time to work out that new piece he had been trying to write out without being hassled if he takes a drink or two for creative purposes. Probably wouldn't hurt to give her a little time alone to think about it. Sweeten her up some.

He stalked off, muttering himself into a fine and righteous anger, woman didn't give him no respect. Somebody was going to have to give and it wouldn't be Luke Bodeen.

The night was chilly and he pulled his collar up around his neck.

Inside Melvira leaned weakly against the door, hurting in spite of herself, trying desperately to step back and put the hoodoo distance on the emotions threatening to overwhelm her. *Heart listen, I am master here.* She sobbed once, a raw ragged sound that filled the empty room but didn't draw tears. He was gone. She walled off the pain and Lucas Bodeen in a cold little dusty corner of her heart. *I am master here.*

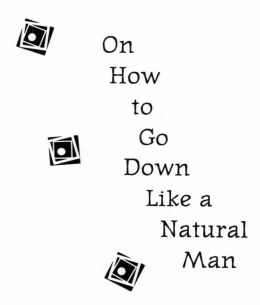

On
How
to
Go
Down
Like a
Natural
Man

WEEK ONE: Bare branches and cool breezes.

The first week or so he ran wild, had himself a real good time. Drank as much as he liked. Picked up on Mamie. Spent a lot of time with the band chasing the blues. Felt good being a free man again, doing what he wanted to do when he wanted to do it. That first weekend he got so tore down drunk it took him two days to recover. Wrote four new blues. Good ones too.

WEEK TWO

The door to the Hole-in-the-Wall opened and let light
in. Lucas Bodeen looked up from his piano. Wasn't Melvira, and he tried to act like he hadn't been looking.

"Don't look like she coming Bodeen," said the Hat.

Bodeen shrugged. He wasn't in the best of moods.
Woman should have been by here by now. She knows
where he works. Know she don't call herself punishing
somebody. Or waiting for him to apologize. Luke Bodeen
don't beg nobody for nothing.

"She'll come." he muttered. He reached for his glass
of brown Tennessee sipping whiskey and drank. Maybe
he should slow down a little. Don't remember the last
time he played straight. Half afraid to. Maybe he would
change his ways. A little. After it was clear who was the
boss.

The door opened and he didn't look up this time. He
listened. Heard the laughter of a couple happy and ready
to party. He started playing again. Hard defiant blues.

"She'll come."

WEEK THREE

Bodeen stood as still and quiet as all the other shadows
in a dark doorway on Hernando. Across the street the
two front windows of their room were dark empty cav-
ities. It was late and Hernando was quiet, with few folk
out. The light of the streetlights didn't reach his hole.
Then she turned the corner and he could suddenly hear
his heart beating. She walked quickly down the street,
all point and purpose, no meandering for his baby.

Watching her made him feel so very soft inside. He fingered the housekey in his hand and fought an urge to go on up to her and apologize, beg, whatever. Nice being a free man, but even nicer to have a woman to come home to. This being a free man just wasn't all that he remembered it being. He wanted to go up to her so bad. Just walk up to her and say, Hey baby, I'm sorry, okay? But if he went back now he would be a whipped man. A wimp. She wouldn't want a chump would she? It'd never be the same. It went against the whole image of himself. Luke Bodeen. Prime goods. Never had to work for a woman in his life. Any woman didn't want to go along with the program could press on. There was always another woman if one started acting up. All he lived for was the music anyway. He always assumed that was what the women liked about him, his cocky give-a-damn attitude. She walked past him and went inside. The light came on in the windows and he stood there for a wavering moment longer before sharply, angrily pulling the collar of his coat up against the crisp onslaught of winter and walking off into the darkness.

I ain't gon do it, he thought, shaking his head, I ain't gon be the one to give.

MONTH ONE

He let himself in. She sat across from the door waiting on him.

Home. His chair, their table, her altar, their bed. The leg on the chair was still broken. She had asked him to fix it, he had meant to, just never got around to it. One of her old beefs. He ignored his packed bags sitting by the door and came over to her like nothings happened, like it hadn't been a month away.

"Hey baby?" he murmered as he kissed her cold cheek and sat on the side of the bed. She didn't respond, didn't hardly move her head. But her eyes watched his every move. He took his shoes off, threw them under the bed, and stretched out.

"So how you been?" he said casually. She didn't reply. Clearly this wasn't going to work. He sat up on the bed.

"You still mad at me huh?"

Still no response, just a flat noncommittal gaze that was worse than being cussed out. He felt the old familiar flareup of the Bodeen temperament and checked himself; he couldn't afford it. He went over to her and put his arms around her, gently pulling her to him. She resisted, standing stiffly in his arms.

"Okay baby, look I was wrong, okay."

"No Lucas," she said flatly, "Not okay. I . . . I just don't feel anything. Not anymore."

Her voice broke and Bodeen's heart lurched. The music was gone. He had forgotten the song of her voice, until just now that it was gone. Her words were flat, "Its been almost a month Bodeen. It was too long. I spent a lot of sleepless nights but now I'm sleeping good again."

She stepped out of his arms; he stepped with her.

"Baby."

The word is hungry, a raw whimpering need. No more ultimatums for Lucas Bodeen, he just wanted to come home. He kissed her hungrily. Or rather at her hungrily; she moved her mouth away. He stiffened, let her go and stepped back.

"Melvira, come on now."

"I need more than you give Bodeen. Probably more than you can give."

He turned cold. He wasn't gon do but so much begging.

"I give what I can," he said.

She looked at him as if seeing somebody she had never seen before.

"Am I important to you?" she asked suddenly, "What's more important to you, me or your work?"

Bodeen was surprised she would ask such a question. He lived to do the blues. His answer was automatic.

"I can't live without my work Melvira, you know that."

She wasn't surprised. Shutters closed down over her eyes and she wasn't there with him anymore. He froze up. And he forgot all about those days of missing her. Forget her. She was threatening the blues.

"I need someone . . ."

He shrugged. He didn't care what she needed.

". . . that I can trust."

Her words were calm and deliberate. Controlled.

"You, you don't want to need anybody do you Bodeen, including me. You didn't mind letting me go, you were relieved. Relieved." She looked at him again with that look that saw him for the first time, with a hurt so deep he looked away.

"You're just spoiled. Women have spoiled you SweetLuke, I spoiled you. You just spoiled."

The tone did it. Another self-righteous judgment. Damn right he was spoiled, and he was supposed to be spoiled. And there were plenty women waiting to spoil him some more.

"Okay baby, if thats the way you want it."

He took his key out of his pocket and put it on a stool beside him. He picked up his bags and he waited, hoping she would panic, break down in tears and beg him to take the key and her back. Nothing. She stood there calm, collected, waiting for him to walk out of her life. He stood there uncomfortably. All he could think of is how he had once been comfortable here. Come in and take those liberties that a man takes with his woman, nuzzle her, handle her. But she wasn't his to hold anymore.

Hey no problem. He was Luke Bodeen. Lady's pet. He's cool. He tipped his hat and he walked out the door. Clearly she wasn't ready.

ONE MONTH TWO WEEKS

Melvira was shopping for vegetables at the Church Park Market when a passing wagon caught her eye. You didn't see that many muledrawn wagons in Memphis these days. She wasn't the only one stopped to watch it meander down Beale, the two mules nervously eyeing the cars and trucks. Two elderly blacks sat up front. A grown boy drove. Two small girls rode behind them. Another family. Another dream. Jah movement of a people.

"Morning Miz Dupree."

The Hootowl, in khaki pants and shirt and carrying

a snakeheaded walking stick. "A little stream," he said, pointing his walking stick at the passing family, "thats part of a mighty river. We wont be a rural people much longer. Its gon cost us though, I give it four, maybe five generations before the dust settle." He shook his head. "Just more figuring to do. Tiresome thing responsibility. Wouldn't you agree Miz Dupree?"

She looked at him and looked away without answering.

"You haven't been by to see me since that first time Dupree. Courtesy call on a fellow practitioner."

The family turned a corner. She looked at him again, held his eye.

"What do you want?"

"I think you might play a role in a trick I got in mind. I believe, you and me, we can alleviate some of the colored race's suffering."

"What are you talking about?" she asked, thoroughly uninterested. "Why me?"

"Who knows why God choose one tool over another."

"God is not what we talking about, we talking about you."

"In this case, I'm confident I speak in God's name."

A older colored man bumped into the Hootowl. Big head that reminded her of another big-headed man. Well dressed but carelessly so, he carried a little black bag in his hand.

"Excuse me Doc," said the Hootowl, doffing his hat.

The old guy frowned when he saw who it was. "Damned hoodoos," he muttered as he walked on by.

"Doc Flowers," the Hootowl told her with that little

infuriating smile of his. "Medical doctor. Went to a fancy
school for it. Finances the colored hospital run by the
Collins Chapel C.M.E. Church over on Ashland with his
own money. Lives down on Pontotoc, white house, red
door. Number Seven-eleven. Easy number to remember,
no? Seven-eleven. A good man, kinda narrow-minded,
but who ain't. He just don't understand that a sick spirit
can kill you just as quick as a sick body. Quicker."

The Hootowl chuckled and his scars danced. He put
his hat back on his head.

He nodded his head, "Good day Miz Dupree," and
took his leave. She watched him weave his way through
the Beale Street crowd, tipping his hat and smiling be-
nevolent blessings on the folks who called out to him.

ONE MONTH THREE WEEKS

He don't care who the boss. He's a miserable man with
something broken inside. Even the blues don't help. One
night it just kinda hit him. He's lost her. He had to face
a life without her. The thought hurt him so bad it was
physical and he had trouble breathing. He put on his hat
and started walking. The morning sun found him at her
door. What was he thinking of when he gave up his key?
Fool. She came to the door, saw who it was through the
screen and shook her head. The door swung shut.

"Melvira."

The door hesitated, stopped, just barely cracked
open. He couldn't see her behind it.

"Melvira?"

"What do you want Lucas?" she asked from behind the cracked door.

"Melvira I just want to talk. Okay? Please."

She opened the door slowly and stood behind the tiny squares of the wire screen, not looking at him, body half turned away.

Bodeen commence to begging. "Baby, look, please, I know I've been a fool about this, okay, I understand now that you the most important thing in my life. Give me another chance baby and I know I can make you happy. I know I can."

Her lip trembled and she shook her head.

"Melvira, I ain't been drinking, I'm willing to . . ."

"Lucas I, I just cant open and close my heart like that, I, I begged you."

"Baby . . ."

"You didn't mind letting me go Bodeen." A tear rolled down her face, the first one he's ever seen. "You didn't put up any fight, you were . . . relieved. You didn't even try to keep me, you didn't want to."

"Aw baby I just want to come home."

Her anger showed. "You were relieved." She turned away. The door closed. He knew then that for her to have gotten to this point meant that she had already killed the love she had had for him. His hardheaded stangaree baby. Something inside of him broke and, still gripping the screen, he slid to his knees, panic rising up in him like vomit he had to keep choking down. He was a wounded animal that wanted nothing more than to die at home.

Mel how could you really leave me?

Never in his life would he have believed a man could hurt like this. His head fell back against the door and he looked up into the sky, one of those grand majestic nights, a haloed full moon, stars so bright you could pluck em, a night just right for talking to God. God help me, please, I ain't never asked you for nothing in my life.

It was a long long night. He ignored the neighbors and the curious stares of the passersby. Forget his pride, he just wanted his woman. He thought about all the times he could have turned it around, when he could have saved himself, saved his life with a word, a move. O Mel how could you really leave me?

He wanted to die, to just lay down and die.

Dawn finally took pity on him. Melvira didn't.

FOUR MONTHS

Go on way from me woman
don't want you no more
go on way from me woman
take your good thing and go.

Bodeen tried. He really did. But he couldn't get her out of his mind. He'd be resolute for a couple of days, a week. Two. Then he'd be back, begging, pleading. Butting his head against the brick wall of her will. And he knew it had become a battle of wills. Her against him. The harder he pushed, the more stubborn she got. But what could he do? He tortured himself with thoughts of some other man holding her, fucking her silly. He heard her whimpering another man's name, saw her writhering under another man. It messed with his head. Bad. Saw it just as clear. Felt the sweat dripping. God help me. He tried to get a hold on himself—You messing with your mind boy, you had it and you blew it, now you just got to be cool and work your way back in.

Made a real pest of himself before finally giving up. When he did give up he gave up on everything. Life without her just wasn't worth the struggle. He filled his days with bad whiskey, hard drugs, long hours and fast women. And he filled his nights with hard and bitter blues.

> *Go on way from me woman*
> *Go on and let me be*
> *Taught me the name of love*
> *But now your name is misery*

SEVEN MONTHS

One night in the Hole-in-the-Wall, low rumbling bass chords reached out and called Mamie. She had been waiting. A big fine righteous woman, and eager to be a good one for Luke Bodeen. Her man of choice. She was ready to please. But Bodeen quickly finds that love is not transferable. He is no longer satisfied just being with a woman, he wants a particular woman. He wants Melvira Dupree in his arms again. Wasn't nobody Melvira but Melvira. Mamie came close, but she didn't reach that barren spot inside. She knew it. You can always tell when somebody is just using you to tread water.

EIGHT MONTHS

Bodeen just sitting there at his piano. Supposed to be a rehearsal, but Bodeen wasn't into it. He was in his own little world and the other guys had just let him sit there while they practiced. They had been real indulgent lately. Bodeen was thinking about Melvira, playing a real slow and sad blues. A crying blues. Suddenly and without warning, hot scalding tears began flowing down his face. And it was like the pain was flowing through his arms through his fingers into the music. And his chest choked up and he threw his head back in a tiny whimper for breath that broke the dam and left him crying raggedly in gasping sobs. He wanted to die, to just lay down and die.

The guys didn't know what to do. They wanted to stop his tears, but they didn't want to interfere with his music. So they just stood there helplessly.

They waited until both subsided. "You all right man?" asked Gabriel. Heavy came up and put his hand on Bodeen's shoulder. "You okay man?"

"Man you need to go get your woman back. Cause you in bad shape."

"Tell me about it. I wish it was that easy."

"Maybe you should take some time off man. Or maybe even get out of town for awhile."

"Leave her?" he asked unbelievingly.

"Ain't doing no good sitting around here crying man."

"Ain't been taking care of yourself either man," Gabriel said, some things that should have been said long before this. "You drinking too much and you got to leave that happy dust alone, you know that stuff ain't good for you man, kills the heart, kills the music. Way too jealous a high for a artist. You know that."

"I got it under control," Bodeen said testily, "quit anytime I like."

"Yeah, how many times have I heard that from a good man going down?"

Gabriel began blowing his harp, his head doing a blind man's radar weave.

"It wont get me."

"Its already got you zombie, you one of the walking dead."

Bodeen shrugged, too drained to argue. He just don't care. It hurt em bad to see him going down like this. Being bluesmen themselves, they had a tendency to live life a little too hard sometimes too. If you want to sing about life, you got to know what you talking about. Everybody know you got to get all down in there if you wanna do the blues. But you cant get lost. They had been real understanding about what Bodeen was going through, but they beginning to worry about their boy. Time to shame him out of it.

"Never thought," said Heavy, "that I'd ever see the day that Luke Bodeen would go down over a woman."

"Hell," said Gabriel, head still weaving, looking intently at the vivid nothing behind his shades, "what else is there to go down over?"

He started singing, almost a hum: "*Every good man need a real good woman, every good . . .*"

Bodeen slammed his keyboard. "Say man, don't you know any other damned songs?"

"Ain't none," said Gabriel, smiling at invisible memories of his own. "That woman musta been your'n, cause you don't miss it like that less it was for you, less'n it was your'n."

Moody wailing harp.

Every good man need . . .

Bodeen put his Stetson on his head and went for the door.

"Bodeen!"

He stopped at the door.

"You don't pull out of this man, we gon have to go on without you."

Bodeen shrugged. "Sure."

He left. They were just too outdone. Going to have to go on without him. When a man determined to go down, especially over a woman, all you can do is hold his coat for him. He might come back for it one day.

TEN MONTHS

Couple of months later, Heavy and the Hat walking through Church's Park over on Fourth and Beale. Church's Park was a special place for the colored community of Memphis, built by Old Man Bob Church because the city didn't allow colored folk into the city parks. Proudful man Old Man Church, did his park up real nice—peacocks, a big auditorium where the Lincoln League met regularly, a carousel in the children's playground. Could meet most anybody up in there. Heavy and the Hat were cutting through it on their way to play at the Hole-in-the-Wall when they saw Luke play-

ing washboard bass. He sat on a stool next to the big
banana tree circled with red and white flowers in the
center of the park. The carousel played a light tune behind them and provided a background to the washboard.
Bodeen rubbed his hands up and down the rough washboard surface reflecting bars of sunlight. A few folk stood
around listlessly. He kept up a equally uninspired patter
going between songs, the grin on his face totally lacking
in dignity.

"Now yall know I pay my rent with this here bass of
mine. Throw some money in the cup. Come on now.
Keep the blues alive."

He stopped often to take a drink from the bottle of
shine in his pocket. A tin can with a few coins in it sat
beside his washtub bass. He looked bad, clothes un-
kempt, half bearded. They felt sorry for him, the mighty
Luke Bodeen brought low. They considered going over,
see if they could do something for him, but they've tried
before. When he stopped to take a break, a couple of
folks dropped coins in the cup at his feet. Some clapped.
As they wandered away he went into the cup and
counted his change. He looked so eager that they were
embarrassed for him and walked away. Bodeen was glad
they went on without bothering him. Didn't feel like
putting up with nobody's bull but his own. Rather just
sit and watch life go by, a shell-shocked spectator, nothing to win, nothing to lose. He pulled at the bottle and
held it up to the light, wondering if he needed to do
another set or if he had enough to get through the night.
It was chilly and he didn't really feel like playing the
cold washboard anymore. He would just have to nurse

what he had. He heard a laugh and looked up to watch a couple pass by, so bundled up in a thick cloak they looked like one person. Sometimes it looked to him that everybody in the world had somebody but him. He took a long swallow, trying to blot out the suddenly surging memories of him and Melvira when it was good, walking through the Sweetwater woods, dancing at the Sweetwater juke, loving all night long. He remembered every gasp, every murmer. He was living more in his memories than his days, memories that had become bright glittering things tainted with sainthood. She had been the best, in all things, in all ways. Boy didn't know whether to bless the day she came into his life or to curse it. He drained his bottle and threw it into the darkness. Curse it. If love meant hurting like this, he didn't want to have anything to do with it.

taught me the name of love
but now your name is misery.

YEAR ONE

Woke up this morning
with the blues walking round my bed.
Went to eat my breakfast
and the blues was all in my bread.

When Bodeen woke up that morning he knew that it was different from any other morning that ever was. For awhile he just laid there feeling bad. Another day to get through. He groped about for a couple of the bot-

tles laying around and held them up to the sunlight coming in through the dingy little window of his dingy little
room. He had killed them all and all he had left was
another day without Melvira. And a hangover. He tossed
and turned for awhile before getting up and finding a
bottle with some dreg at the bottom. He turned it up,
letting the warm liquor dripdrop to his tongue. That got
him started. He collected every bottle with a corner of
liquor left and slowly, carefully, poured the dregs from
different liquors into one glass until it was about a
quarter full. As he worked he noticed himself in a
busted-up old mirror leaning against the wall. Left by
the last drunk to rent the little room across from the
Beale Street Baptist Church. Pieces of it were missing,
like a jigsaw puzzle, and the busted reflection separated
his head from his body. He laughed, a low sour laugh.
A him with pieces missing. A head with no body. Or
would it be a body with no head? He watched himself
take a sip of his concoction, or watched it rather, the
head. It grimaced. He didn't blame it; the stuff was
strong. He took another sip and frowned, thick eyebrows
drawing together over deepset eyes. Cause the more he
looked at the head in the mirror, the less he felt like
laughing. It looked bad, puffy, the skin hanging loose
off the bone. Bloated, eyes rimmed and red. Was that
really him? Looks bad Bodeen, real bad.

Still sipping, he looked around the filthy little room.
Through the dirty window he could see the statue of
John the Baptist on top of the Beale Street Baptist
Church. The morning shadow reached his room. He
looked around at the bottles and the spent happy dust

tins. The bloated head in the mirror. And all he could think was—I was a man once.

He sighed, a deep and heavy sigh. Looks like my baby just mighta knew what she was doing when she left me. When she jumped a sinking ship. He sucked his tooth in disgust, phwwwwt, a habit he had picked up from her. Look like she was right about the high, too, turned on him first chance it got.

Now, in spite of having lived with a conjure woman all this time, Luke Bodeen didn't really believe in that hoodoo thing. At least not for him. Didn't believe in signs and all that kind of stuff. But just then, just when he needed to hear it, he heard the faint wail of a passing train. He listened, he listened real hard, a delta freight train calling his name. He's sitting there and he's thinking what do I have to show for 38 years of life? I've lost it all. If I died tomorrow who would know? No woman. No band. No self-respect. No rep. Even Mamie had gave up on him, turned her head when she saw him in the street. His face screwed up as he fought the urge to cry.

He looked at the bottle of muddy liquor in his hand and set it down. He was tired of hurting.

I was a man once.

He stood and stretched. A good bone-popping stretch. Well, my friend, I spec its time to pick your chin up off the ground. My friend, its time to go. He washed up, first time this week, and groomed himself best he could. Then he put his still crisp Stetson on his head, took up that last bottle and walked on down to the river. At the river he stood and savored it for a moment. Been gone too long ain't I old friend? He stood there for awhile just letting it talk to him, watching it flow past slow and steady. Him and that old river, they come a long long way. He started to drink the last of the dregs from the bottle in his hand. One last time. But theres always that one last time, isn't it? He turned the bottle up and poured it into the river. A libation to what was and what ought to be. Melvira would have liked that little touch.

I'm gone baby, you take care of yourself now.

He flung the bottle in and walked back up the bluff. One thing a good bluesman got to know. When its time to go its time to go.

A woman gets the blues,
she hangs her head and cries.
A man gets the blues
he grabs a freight train and rides.

He felt lightheaded that night, waiting on the 12:05 near the railroad tracks up near the old slaveblocks on Auction Square. The tracks bent here and the train had to slow down. Didn't want to go. Lord knows he didn't. Leaving town was like giving up. There wouldn't be any chance of getting her back now. He snorted, hmmph, like he had a chance anyway. If he stayed he was just going to keep on going down. He thought sourly that he hoped she missed him. Hoped life broke her stiff little back. Then he smiled in spite of himself, a smile that remembered when she loved him, No, he didn't wish her no aggravation. He hoped she found all she wanted, including a man that made her happy. My baby. My sweet stangaree baby.

He's traveling light, everything he owns he's carrying. The night was quiet and he was glad he was the only one out, didn't feel like conversation or even wariness. He was just too tired. He was so busy feeling sorry for himself that he didn't hear the train until it was right up on him, slowing down for the bend. Well Bodeen, I guess thats it. He began trotting alongside it. Suddenly he stopped and looked back at the glow of downtown Memphis. She would be asleep, on her back, arms thrown around her head, that thick crop of hair that he liked to nuzzle in framing her face. Her hair always smelled like morning to him. My baby. Suddenly he had trouble breathing, had to open his mouth wide and take deep ragged breaths. The wind of the passing train tugged at him and he thought about trying one more time. She might be sitting there right now, waiting for him to try that one more time.

The train whistled, almost past him, and he started running. Had to sprint for it, shoes digging into the sliding gravel of the trackbed until he had his speed, grabbed a ladder rail and swung himself up into an empty boxcar. Didn't feel like riding the blinds tonight; tonight he was going first class. He sat for a minute on the lip of the door, gasping for breath and sweating liquor. The breeze felt like it was stripping a year's worth of worriation from his face. He felt a little like the old Bodeen again, just a little. Should've done this a year ago. He slid back to the boxcar wall opposite the open door. The vibration felt good to his back, and he scrunched up enough straw to make himself comfortable. Outside the darklined silhouette of the delta landscape ran past the boxcar doors and he savored the feel of movement and the rhythmatic clacking of a train making goodtime, a sound that has soothed him since he was a child. Specially in quietnight. So he's sitting there and he's waiting to feel good, but all he's feeling is empty and he's looking back at the lights of Memphis growing dim and he feels like crying. Probably did. Who was going to take care of her? Who was going to love her right?

"Bye baby," he heard himself murmer at the fading lights, "cant be in the same town with you and not want you. I gotta go."

Melvira woke in the night and turned away from the light of the full moon shining through her front window. She would miss him after all.

She slept restlessly that night, her traveling spirit kept tightly leashed. On her way to market the next morning she noticed yet another colored family in transit, bags and children close at hand. A young couple with two little kids who could barely walk. He in starched and pressed overalls, she in a frilled calico that had to be her Sunday best. Melvira stopped and stared, curiously stirred by the strong emanations left in their wake. Her hoodoo sense of significance alert, she followed them down Main Street to the Illinois Central train station. The closer they got to the imposing whitestone building, the more crowded the streets were, filled with colored folk converging on the train station, many of them families like the ones she followed. As she became part of the flow of humanity she felt as if she were part of some tribal movement, a migration to better pastures or fleeing an implacable enemy. Inside the huge building was chaos, hustling redcaps, people waiting in line and on benches, all kinds of emotions in their faces and postures, hope, patience, sadness, joy, determination. Some hid their emotions behind expressions so ruthlessly blank that it was as if they were hiding them from themselves rather than others. Colored families, some clearly off the farm for the first time in their lives, grouped together in nervous little defensive knots for protection, fast-lane city slickers hovering around them like vultures sensing fresh meat. All around her, she heard tearful goodbyes. "You go to that mailbox everyday now baby. Soon as I get a job I'ma send for you and the girls. Aw come on baby, don't cry on me, I can't go if its gon to make you cry."

As she watched an emotion that has been lurking around the fringes of her consciousness began to build in her. A sadness, a regret, a guilt that grew in her as if this all were in some way her fault. As if there was something she could and would not do.

The conductor came through the waiting room, calling out almost in her ear, "All aboard! All aboard! All aboard the northbound train!" The crowd surged toward the gate and Melvira felt tears rolling down her cheek. Her sad beautiful people. Turning to leave, she had to blindly fight her way against the surging tide.

Way back when, when the earth was young and the dreams began, the old teller of tales found the tribe's

witch woman beneath the sacred baobab tree. He sat
and waited for her to acknowledge his presence. They
were the tribe's oldest members, these two, and it had
been decided that she might listen to him. He shifted
impatiently; the tribe may have left them both.

"We must go soon," he said finally. "To stay is the
death of the Tribe. If our generations are to prosper we
must go. It was you who pointed this out to them."

She didn't answer.

"They will leave you."

She looked at him with eyes that did not see him. In
a dark and turbulent sky, thunder rumbled quietly.
Oluddumare's song.

"I am old and rooted here," she said presently. "I
cannot go. I will not go. My power is here."

The teller of tales rose with joints that ached more
each winter and told the tribe she would not come. The
Council of Elders went into conference. There were
those who would not leave without her. There were
those who voted good riddance to a troublesome old
busybody. Yet on one thing they all agreed, and when
the tribe was ready to move a stretcher made from the
hide of a great tusked one was sent and, in spite of her
protests, the old woman was placed upon it. It had been
decided that she could not be left. A tribe without its
vision master was naked before both its enemies and
the gods.

The Hootowl knocked on her door around high noon.

"Well Miz Dupree," he said with a nod of his gray

head when she came to the door, "ready for instruction?"

She frowned and he tapped his snake-headed walking cane on the porch, "I don't suppose Miz Dupree that you thinking of ignoring a calling. Don't want the gods to turn on you now, they been looking on you with particular favor."

When still she hesitated, he added, "In the interest of furthering your understanding."

Knowledge, Understanding, Power, Enlightenment, Wisdom. The hoodoo hungers. Plus that she was curious.

"Just a moment Mr. Hootowl, I'll be right with you."

She draped herself in white and placed a wide straw hat on her head. A fast learner, the Melvira Dupree who stepped out to join the Hootowl no longer resembled the country girl who had come to Memphis just two years ago with her mouth open. She was so at home on Beale now that she had even adopted a style. She always wore white; fresh, clean whites, liking the feel of it and aware of the drama it added to her act. White shawls flowing from her shoulders and carrying a string bag in case she decided to go shopping for fruits and vegetables, she followed him through the lunchhour streets, pacing herself to the Hootowl's short old man's steps. Folks stared. The Hootowl rarely walked the streets of Memphis, preferring to stay aboard his houseboat and have folks come to him. Passersby that knew him pointed him out to those that didn't.

Melvira Dupree liked the Hootowl in spite of her instinctive resistance to those who would use her as a tool in their own spells. Though as yet unmoved, she was intrigued by this inclination of her hoodoo elders to see in her something special. She looked on the Hootowl like a meddlesome but benign neighbor who could be safely indulged.

"I think this will be an interesting evening for you Miz Dupree," said the Hootowl.

With affection had come irreverence, the droll humorous side she showed only to the two or three people on the planet she called friend. "Getting my interest ain't near as hard as holding it," she told him.

He chuckled, relishing the challenge. "Well let me try this one on you Miz Dupree. Ever hear of Oluddumare?"

"No," she said, "can't say that I have."

"A African name for God. What they call the High God. The big mojo of the spiritworld. What about Shango? Legba? Yemanya? Oshun? Obatala? Ogun? Babalu?"

The names of Hoodoo Maggie's cats. Spirits the old lady had always called on in her work.

"The Seven African Powers," said Melvira Dupree.

The Hootowl beamed approval of good training and congratulated himself again on his own vision. He had chosen well. Melvira, of course, knew little more than that Hoodoo Maggie had called her cats by those names, said they was names of powerful African spirits and they were the oldest and most powerful spirits of all. Beyond that they meant little to her. Africa itself meant little to her.

Oluddumare. She let her soul taste it and she judged it sweet and spiritually satisfying.

"In other countries of the America's you got black-folks what worship black gods."

She frowned eloquently. Such talk disturbed her. In spite of her hoodoo training, if you pushed her to the wall she would declare that there is but one God and Jehovah is His name. Or Allah. Or even better, the Father, Son and the Holy Ghost.

"Mythology Miz Dupree," scoffed the Hootowl, "outdated mythology at that. You don't really think God is some bearded whiteman sitting on a golden throne in heaven do you? Much less three of Them. God aint no He and God aint no She. God is a great big It, God the Universe, and if that bother you then I'm sorry for you. Humanfolk have always seen their Gods in their own image, somebody you can talk too. Its a natural thing. But God is much more than that Miss Dupree, more than we can ever name. And what I'm saying to you that the African way of seeing God is as valid as the one you using now. Blackfolks in Brazil, the Caribe Islands, Africa, they got a African way of knowing God. They still got God in they hoodoo. Here in the states the old gods are forgotten. Too strong to out-and-out die, they remain only as spirits. And we who were once holy are now only sorcerors." His voice was bitter with unwanted knowledge.

"There are many ways to God," she said. A rote declaration to cover her uneasiness.

"Indeed. You must go and visit these other colored folks one day and know what they know."

"You presume," she murmered, balance regained.

"Indeed I do," he replied, his good humor unabated.

He stopped. They were in front of Jackson's Drug Store.

"Here we are," he said, "one of my sources of power."

Obviously a private little joke. The old man was in a good mood.

Jackson's Drug Store was a small venerable establishment that Melvira had often passed in her travels up and down Beale. Though she wondered what kinds of herbs and medicines they stocked in a Drug Store, she had never entered it, feeling as if they were in some way the competition.

At that time Jackson's Drug Store was the premier gathering hole of Beale Street's resident intellectuals. They gathered there daily to discuss the issues of the day and the appropriate strategic responses of the colored world. The topics discussed and the participants of any given day varied, but during lunch hour a hard core of regulars could be expected. Three regulars were there and in full-throated argument when the Hootowl and Melvira Dupree walked in. They were sitting in the back of the store where Jackson mixed his apothecary connections and waited on customers, who would often join in the discussions while waiting on their prescriptions. Casey, the Beale Street postman, and young Dr. Blassingame, whose office was right down the street, were, as usual, in contention. When Melvira and the Hootowl walked in, they barely looked up. Only Miss Martha Rush, another regular and a teacher at LeMoyne Normal, the local colored college, acknowledged them with a nod.

When the old rootdoctor first started coming to their

lunch hour discussions, they had been immensely curious. The rootdoctor never participated though, would find himself a chair and listen quietly to the discussions raging around him. Judicious questions designed to draw him out received discouraging monosyllabic answers. For awhile hoodoo and hoodoo doctors had become a primary issue of discussion, when he wasn't there of course. There were those, Miss Rush for one, who claimed that hoodoo represented a fundamental drive of the colored race. But the others could not for the life of them see what value magic and magicworkers had for the Negro struggle. If anything, it was agreed, hoodoo was embarrassing, outdated behavior that weakened the colored race and should be allowed to die off at first opportunity.

The fourth person of the group wasn't a regular, an impressive woman in bold brownskin features, a pillbox hat sitting confidently over high bangs and a feathered boa draped carelessly around her neck. She sat somewhat apart from the others, listening intently, occasionally taking notes in a spiral notebook.

The Hootowl took a seat near the newcomer. Melvira lingered, fascinated with the shelved medicines, once again slapped in the face with her ever-growing lack of knowledge of the way of things in this world.

Casey and Blassingame picked up where they had left off. "For an educated man, you sure are a fool doc."

"W-why am I a f-f-fool because y-y-you don't k-know what you talking about Casey?" He took gold-rimmed spectacles off and wiped them meticulously. A starched white highcollar bracketed the dark chiseled features of his face. He rarely smiled. It was his stutter that endeared him to his patients and exasperated his fellow disputants.

"I do so know what I'm talking about Doc. Marcus Mosiah Garvey is the anointed savior of the blackman."

Casey was a card-carrying member of the United Negro Improvement Association. Neither Garvey's failed UNIA businesses nor his arrest on mail fraud had dimmed Casey's regard. Dr. Blassingame, a member of the Lincoln League and president of the local NAACP, was a firm follower of Dr. Du Bois. "Garvey is a buffoon sir, an embarrassment. Provisional President of Africa, indeed. Our struggle is here."

"Uh huh Doc, even your precious Du Bois fella recognizes the importance of Africa. Convened those Congress what tried to get the colonial powers out of Africa. Didn't get nowhere though did he, because he don't understand that you have to talk to whitefolks face to face, from a position of power. Garvey ain't asking them for nothing. The blackman will provide."

Miss Rush took that opportunity to comment that all this talk about Africa was well and good, but what did it do to help the plight of colored people here in Memphis, of the blackman that got lynched just the other Saturday in Brownsville. What we needed, she declared, is ten more Ida B. Wells.

Ida was one of colored Memphis's favorite daughters, and both Casey and Blassingame knew better than to speak against her directly.

"Hmph," growled Casey, "and they ran her out of town on a rail. Burnt her paper down and ran her out of town. Thats because she didn't have the power of Africans all over the world to back her up. There's black-folk all around the world and one day we will be one people."

"What power?" snorted Blassingame.

"The power of a people with a destiny," snarled Casey.

"Relax Casey," laughed Blassingame. "N-Next thing I-I know you'll be conjuring l-l-like our conjure friend h-here."

At this point the woman in the boa put her pen down and leaned forward into the conversation.

"Who, you?" she asked the Hootowl, "are you a con-jure man?"

The Hootowl nodded once. "Some folks call me so. Yourself?"

"Zora Neale Hurston," she answered with an infec-tiously lopsided grin and a habitual flick of her boa. "I'm down here visiting my brother Ben. I'm a writer and I'm studying to be an anthropologist. I'm considering trav-eling around the south recording the culture of the col-ored people as part of my studies. I've thought about interviewing hoodoos and conjures as part of it. Are you really a conjure?"

"He sure is mam," said Casey, "considered the High Hoodoo round these parts I'd say."

"The High Hoodoo?"

"The big man, mam, the king of the hoodoos. Mem-phis has always had a High Hoodoo that the others ones look up to."

She turned back to the Hootowl, brown eyes blazing. "Are you?"

"I consider myself a knowledgeable man," murmered the Hootowl with a polished humility.

"And you?" She turned to Melvira, equally excited. Melvira, more used to boasting and showtalking to convince clients of her power, instead followed the Hootowl's noncommittal lead. "I turn a trick or two."

Zora Neale scribbled that down, eyes not leaving Melvira, as if the conjure woman might disappear if she blinked. "Do you come here often? Why are you here?"

"Instruction," answered Melvira with an amused look at the Hootowl. A puzzled Zora Neale also looked at the Hootowl.

"Power," said the Hootowl.

"Real difficult to get a straight answer out of a hoo-doo, mam," volunteered Casey.

"Y-Y-Y-you don't really want to w-w-write about that oldtimey stuff do you Miss uh Hurston?"

Far as they were concerned if Ben Hurston's little sister was going to write about colored Memphis they didn't want to leave her with the impression that they were backwards down here. Next thing you know she would be calling them Bubba.

"Just what," asked the Hootowl, "do you plan to say about the hoodoo way Miss Hurston?"

"Won't know till I study it," she said flippantly. "I do believe, though, that the Negro culture has something to give the world."

"I agree, b-b-b-but one that has been re-re-refined and made suitable for the twentieth century. W-w-we have to l-look ahead, not backwards."

"Diluted don't you mean Doc?"

That started them off again. Zora took the opportunity to scoot her chair closer to Melvira. This Melvira Dupree intrigued her. She didn't fit Zora Neale's idea of a conjure woman. The clear brown eyes regarding her were open and without subterfuge. And way too attractive. It was only after she had looked closely that Zora recognized the amusement that had also been in the eyes of the really good conjures she had known back home in Florida.

Melvira was equally intrigued. It would be easy to give her a reading, thought Melvira, a woman with a destiny, her fate lies close to the surface.

"How come you to be a hoodoo?" asked Zora.

"How come you to be a writer?" asked Melvira.

They were too much alike not to try each other. They had everybody's attention now, two strong women, each determined to be the question and not the answer. Zora, worldly and already jaded, Melvira, a provincial country hoodoo with a lot to learn. Yet they recognized in each other sisters of the cloth. Melvira's lips twitched with a pleasure she couldn't hide and was answered with one of Zora's unrestrained grins and a laugh that made everybody smile and chuckle along with her. She put away both pad and pen.

"How come you to be a hoodoo?" she asked, genuinely curious.

It was difficult for Melvira Dupree to give a straight answer. Signification is the hoodoo way. But if Zora put away her tools, Melvira would too. Even still, she surprised herself when she said, "Because my mother was before me. I've been a hoodoo since I was a girl. Possibly since I was born. Do you really write books?"

"I write. I plan to write books. Good ones too. Immortal ones."

She smiled, and Melvira's heart went out to her. "Books on hoodoo?"

Zora hesitated. She had thought about it, but hadn't really decided. Uncomfortable in the unfamiliar role of interviewee of one of her folks subjects, she pulled out her pen and held it in her hand.

"Yes," she said, decision suddenly made. "Yes I will. Can you help me? Can I interview you?"

Melvira stared at Zora Neale like other folks stared at her when she walked the streets of Memphis, trying to see what made her what she was. Melvira hadn't really thought about coloredfolks as writers. Her reading consisted of the Bible and the newspapers that the Hootowl often asked her to read to him. The thought of writing books on hoodoo was totally new to her and, once again, she could only wonder at her lack of understanding. So much world to know. If the hoodoo world was dependent on her, it was in big trouble.

"Why hoodoo?" Casey demanded of Zora Neale.

"Why not hoodoo," said Miss Rush softly. "Both of them work with the soul."

"W-W-w-what?"

"Literature and hoodoo," she said, "both are tools for shaping the soul."

"Spiritwork," said the Hootowl. "Sacred literature."

The regulars glanced at each other with expectant surprise. They weren't used to the Hootowl volunteering participation. He never spoke. Never. And they could tell from the way his face was lit up that they were about to get a glimpse beyond the mask.

"Spiritwork," he said with a nod of acknowledgment to Miss Rush. "If you would provide tribal guidance, you must work with the tribal soul." Casey frowned. "Stay with me," said the Hootowl. "Strategies now, they change with time and circumstance. Each makes it contribution in its proper time and place. But if you want to have fundamental influence on the colored race's destiny, you shape its soul and the soul shapes everything else. Rootwork."

"Tell me Mr. uh Hootowl," asked Zora, again pulling out her pad and pen, "why aren't you a Christian? There's a lot of good in Christianity, do you agree?"

"Absolutely." The Hootowl nodded affably.

"And coloredfolks trust it a heap more than they do hoodoo. It would be an easier road to walk. Why hoodoo?"

"Because," said the Hootowl, "the hoodoo way is our slice of Godhome. Whatever we have kept of our African soul we have kept in hoodoo. The soul of a human race born in Africa. And the only way it and the African way grows, evolves and continues to serve us is when those of us with power choose to serve it."

The Hootowl had been born a slave on the last day of the Civil War. Came by hoodooing honestly; his daddy was a hoodoo before him, as were his six uncles and his six older brothers. His daddy and his brothers trained him from birth. First thing he remembered in life was his daddy telling him that the only inviolate rule of hoodoo is Anymethod Anytime.

He didn't take up hoodooing himself until after he came back from the sea. Went to sea because his daddy told him it behooved a young man to see the world while he was still young and before his responsibilities tied him down. Shipped out as a cabinboy when he was 15 and traveled up and down the Americas from Maine to Brazil for over 10 years, and he thanked his daddy for it every day. Saw more of life than a colored man was ever supposed to see in those days.

It was in Brazil that he first learned of blackfolks hoodooing a different kind of hoodoo. Was living with a woman whose practices hummed on his memory strings. He recognized the herbs she mixed, the bowl of white cleansing liquid she poured on his head when he entered her life, the steady stream of clients that she advised. Conjure woman, he thought with a smile, he would pick a conjure woman. It triggered all the hoodoo training of his childhood. When asked, she told him that she was a Macumba priestess. He went with her to the terriero and was totally fascinated. His fascination peaked when Myrena, standing serenely by his side and listening to the drums, suddenly jerked into life and danced out into the swaying drumdriven crowd of worshippers. Iemanja had mounted her, she explained to him that night. All about him the gods had mounted their horses and spoke in tongues. He went as often as he could, but he refused to salute the leaders by laying on his belly. Just wasn't his style. He was an American, from Tennessee, USA, he would explain; he didn't lay down on his belly for nobody. I can't imagine such a thing. He also refused, in spite of her repeated exhortation, to submit to the touch of the gods. He was from a family and a culture of sorcerors who didn't acknowledge anybody or anything greater than themselves. Wouldn't be rode by man or god. He was constantly asking her why did they do certain rituals, why certain beliefs. The answer that it has always been that way, or that the gods demand it, did not impress him. He explained that hoodoos demand to know the whys of all things. When she understood his refusal to be bound by their rules and became aware of his sudden growth in power, she put him out. One sorceror per household is more than enough.

But his eyes were open now, and he began to note the African religions in different ports of call in the Americas. He attended voodoo rites in Haiti, Santeria ceremonies in Cuba, Obeah rituals in Jamaica, and any others he could find. The more he was exposed to the extent of the African Way in the New World, the prouder he became of being a hoodooman. He realized that he was part of a family of African religions and, though clearly hoodoo had lost more of its religious power than any of the others, neither was it burdened with outdated religious dogma and mythology. His contempt for African fears of spiritharm were as fundamental as his disdain for burning in hell forever. Totally reject bloody animal sacrifice. Anathema. This does not please the gods. Better good deeds, flowers, candles, drums and righteousness. It was in Brazil that he first heard the blessing, *"Oluddumare mojuba."* African words, explained Myrena, a friend now, "God's blessings on us all."

That got him curious about Africa, and he signed on

to a ship going to Angola. Didn't spend but a hour ashore, but it was the most important hour of his life. The minute he stepped on African soil he felt his guardian spirits grow in power. Until then he had felt like most colored-folk of his time about Africa, a sorry blighted place that you wouldn't want to even visit, much less live. When he left he had tribal scars carved into his cheek and his Fa was strong in his soul. It was his last trip aboard. He never went to sea again. Came back to the states a full-grown sorceror in his prime, totally confident of his power and his training. A profoundly arrogant man who effortlessly carved out a place for himself in the cut-throat voodoo world of New Orleans. Can't be a sorcerer of any note unless you're totally convinced that you are the strongest power on the planet. That it is in your mind and will that true reality is born and nurtured, and that all other realities must yield to you and the hoodoo will. Mangod.

Ravenous with the hunger of the sorcerer for power of any sort, spiritual, personal and temporal, he system-atically drew strands of power unto himself until he was a bloated spider in the middle of a web of power that responded to his every twitch. It was in New Orleans that he learned the value of a good information network. It was Marie Leveaux the Elder that taught the hoodoo world that there is no power like that of a well-used secret.

His reputation for true wisdom and his pride in being a hoodoo in a voodoo town named him the Hoodoo Hoot-owl. Outside of his scars, he disdained the trappings and the drama that lesser hoodoos used to awe the gullible.

He knew that the strength of a conjure depends on the amount of metaphysical understanding that the worker has, and he applied himself diligently to understanding the way of things. Striving to be a competent practitioner of the mystical sciences. Like his daddy had taught him, he wasn't bound by any rules. He used whatever tech worked—Anymethod Anytime.

At the top of his game but curiously jaded, he left New Orleans on a northbound riverboat with a vague hunger for something else. Exactly what he didn't know. The voodoo world of New Orleans was as set in its ways as any of the others he had known, and already he sensed the musty smell of an outdated game. Though he didn't realize it at the time, he was weary of the spiritual stuntage his ruthless struggle for sorceric power entailed. You lose human compassion when you constantly trying to manipulate everybody in your ever expanding sphere of influence, when, as he often told himself with the same satisfaction that came from eating a good meal, "everybody on the planet works for me. Whether they know it or not."

So when his Fa suggested he leave, he did so without complaint or a backwards glance. His guardian spirit had never yet let him down. Didn't know where he was going, but when he reached Memphis he knew he was there. *Holyground,* his Fa murmured when he walked off the riverboat with a strong, almost mystical sense of being finally home, *Holyground.*

He built his houseboat because he missed the sea. Used driftwood because he liked the feel of movement and life it gave, the way it made him and his boat a natural part of the river.

He married once, a fellow conjuror and the only person he ever met who was stronger than he was. Softer too. He loved her more than life, and it was only when she died in spite of all that he could do that he realized there were in truth greater powers than himself. It was then that he truly turned to God and the sorcerer became the prophet.

Doc Hootowl spent the rest of his years preparing for the call he knew would someday come. He was an old man before he found what he was looking for. It came to him gradually, as the sleepy little rivertown grew into a city and spread away from the river and the attitude of coloredfolks toward hoodoo changed. As they became a more cosmopolitan people, what they had once feared and respected they now considered a joke and an embarrassment.

Over the years his thriving hoodoo business fell off, as did that of the lesser hoodoos who once thronged the Memphis streets. He watched the Work deteriorate into spiritual and magical hucksterism, and he pondered on this long and hard. He was there when the great migration off the farms and fields of the delta began and he watched it grow from a small trickle to a mighty flood, wondering if the hoodoo way would be left behind with the mules and outhouses of the delta. The race was getting far too sophisticated for his kind of hoodoo. They took their bodies to the doctor and their souls to the preacher. Considered becoming a Baptist preacher himself once. But he felt with all his heart that the colored race deserved a spiritual tradition of its own. Needed one desperately. He knew that if the hoodoo way was to remain valid, it would have to find new life and purpose.

It didn't come together for him until the day he saw Melvira Dupree reading her Bible after leaving church one bright pretty Sunday morning. His sources had already informed him of her. New hoodoo in town and, most important, he knew that she did good work. A true hoodoo of considerable power. Standing there watching her read her Bible was like a revelation. Like many coloredfolks of his day and time he had never learned how to read, a power he had never mastered. Now that he understood the power of being able to read when other folks couldn't, he was just too old to try. But this Dupree, possibly this was the new style hoodoo that would save the hoodoo way. In her he saw the future and the future was good.

He had been feeling the bitter bite of his days lately and had begun to fear that all the knowledge and understanding he had bought so dearly with the coin of his lifeyears would die out with him. He saw in Melvira Dupree his last chance to serve the colored race. He monitored her. He sent agents in for consultations and received his reports—true power, true vision, true compassion. She was the one.

Oluddumare mojuba.

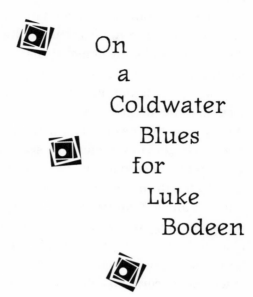

On
a
Coldwater
Blues
for
Luke
Bodeen

Ole Bodeen went home when he left Memphis, looking for a hole where he could lick his wounds. He slept well, soothed by that steady train rhythm and the miles rolling by outside the boxcar door. The sun was just rising by the time the train passed the family farm. He could see it as soon as the train made the bend, a little shotgun house weathered gray and nestled in flat brown cottonland stretching to the horizon.

When the train slowed he jumped down and made his way down the hill. How many times had he come down that hill coming home? He had grown up watching freights pass by on that hill. Caught his first freight when he was 9, left home on the Memphis bound when he was 15. Came home every three, four years or so. Never stayed over two weeks. The first week would be fine, everybody glad to see him. The second one he'd be fidgety, and his momma would be tired of picking up after him. By the third week he was gone. He came down the hill with an old familiar smile that got wider and wider. But something was wrong this time. At first he couldn't place it. He was almost at the little shotgun house before he realized what it was. No crop. Nothing. No hogs, no chickens, no corn, no collards, potatoes or watermelon. The farm wasn't alive. He had never seen it like this, not this time of year. He started dragging his feet some. This wasn't good. Smoke came from the chimney so he knew somebody was home. The little weathered house sat high on its delta stilts, stubby brick columns that rose the house off the ground and out of highwater. Small covered porches bookended it. Beneath the front porch a old yella houndog panted and thumped his tail. The sound of Bodeen's boots on the porchwood caused the tail to thump harder.

The screen door was unlocked, he walked in. He walked through the frontroom to the kitchen. His momma sat at the table shelling green peas into a crockery bowl, stripping the long green shells away in one clean deliberate motion. He watched her a moment.

Elder Bodeen. A gentle set woman whose long hard life on the delta didn't show on her, shelling the peas with the slow deliberateness that was a part of everything she did. She looked up unsurprised. "Thought I heard a train go by just now."

They were used to his wandering ways.

"Hey ma, allright if come home for awhile?"

She had stood to take her coming home hug, but that awkward question caused her to stop and look at him. Her eyes crinkled in disapproval at the shape he's in. He shifted uncomfortably. Last time he came home he had been flush, money in his pocket and a gleam in his eye. He could almost hear the questions growing in her mind.

"You already home ain't you?"

"Thanks ma." He hugged her and sat down at the kitchen table, still conscious of her eyes on him. She wouldn't press him for an explanation just yet. That he needed to come home was sufficient.

"Where you been this time?"

"Chicago mostly. Traveled with a medicine show for awhile. Spent a year in Arkansas . . . met a woman there."

He tried to keep the pain out of his voice, but she knew him too well.

"I hope you treated her better than you treated the others."

He wanted to tell it all. "No," he said, finally, "no, I guess I didn't."

"Obviously," she said, "else you'd be there instead of here."

It was time to face the hammer. Momma was a soft

touch; Big Lucas would ask questions and pass judgments. He sighed. Might as well get it over with. He just hated for his daddy to see him like this.

"Where's daddy?"

"Uh, Luke, things a little different since the last time you were here."

She sounded strained. He waited, refusing to think it. Daddy was forever. He remembered that he meant to ask about the farm.

"Momma . . ."

"Your daddy hasn't been well."

He relaxed; not well wasn't bad, he hadn't been well either.

"Whats wrong momma?"

She didn't look at him. "He don't get around like he used to—he's had a couple of strokes and uh . . ."

Bodeen didn't want to deal with it. He felt antsy and wanted to leave, change the subject.

"Tired," she said, "he's just tired Luke."

He couldn't possibly be tireder than she sounded. "Whats wrong momma?"

"He tired Lucas and he just don't know how to quit."

"Somebody shoulda told me," he accused.

"How exactly were we supposed to get in touch with you? Every two or three years I look up and see you coming down the hill."

Though there was no accusation in her voice, he felt chastised. "All right to go see him?"

"If he sleeping don't wake him."

He went to their room, last room in the house. At first he didn't recognize the little old man lying there so limply in the bed. His hair was wispy and his skin hung loosely off thin little bones. Daddy was a big man, bigger than life, a force of nature. Big Luke Bodeen. Eternal like the seasons that he lived and worked by. Bodeen stood there in the doorway with his mouth open. Daddy? This shallow little replica of the man he knew just three, four years ago. Little Luke backed out.

Back in the kitchen his momma was waiting, peas unshelled in her hands. He sat down across from her.

"He was just suddenly old," she said after a moment, an emotionless pre-prepared statement for a question she had known was coming. "Three strokes so far. Just drove himself too hard. Never did have as much respect for himself as he did for this land."

"He was sleeping," Luke said lamely. She had put some grits and biscuits on. He went to the pot of grits boiling on the stove and looked in hungrily; been a long-time since he ate right.

His momma watched him, again shelling the long green peas in her hand with a steady rhythm, "What was her name, the woman in Arkansas?"

"How is Luann and Martin?"

"Your sister and her husband just moved onto Dock-ery land east of here. She was down just yesterday. She come fairly regular. She'll be glad to see you. They strug-gling but who ain't. They just got another boy, that makes three. Mart still in Chicago. Came home about a year ago last Christmas and brought his youngest. He doing well. Always did. What was her name?"

"I don't want to talk about her momma."

He was sitting at the table, sopping grits with his

biscuits, when his daddy came out in a T-shirt and faded, well-patched overalls.

He nodded "Morning boy," as though Bodeen hadn't been gone all these years. No surprise, no questions. His old man sat down in slow and careful stages, and Lucas had this sudden surge of raw affection. Momma helped him sit and tucked a napkin under his chin. Daddy, who had always been the boss, the strong one in the family, docilely getting a bib tucked under his chin. Much as he didn't want to answer questions, he didn't like this; his daddy had always been a curious man. He reached out and touched his daddy's bony shoulder, all the love in the world in the gesture. "Hey daddy." Watching his daddy eat, Bodeen is suddenly aware of just how little he knew of the man sitting across from him. He had been on the road since he was 15, a traveling man, always coming home after being long gone and always at least four or five years behind in his knowledge of his father. All his life his father has been snapshots frozen in time. This time the snapshot was so sepia old and faded you could hardly see it. Lucas's eyes watered and he concentrated on his grits. Surreptitiously he watched his daddy eat, such slow careful movement of his spoon to his mouth. Just feeding himself seemed such a chore that when his daddy put on his old redflannel working shirt, at first Lucas didn't realize the significance of it. "You going to work daddy?"

His daddy looked offended. "Sun ain't stopped shining have it, a man don't stop working."

Bodeen's momma looked at him like, Why don't you try, he may listen to you.

Like anybody could get daddy to do what he didn't
feel like doing. He may be old and tired but he was still
Daddy.

"Daddy you not still trying to work the farm are you?"

"How else it gon get worked? Whats wrong with
you boy?"

He shuffled toward the door. Bodeen stood and
caught up with him. "Guess I might as well earn my
keep."

In the barn a mule stood in the stall, a big gray, easily
a thousand pounds or better. "Hey boy." Lucas twitched
Booker T's drooping left ear, and the old mule nudged
him affectionately. Booker T had been in the family for
at least ten years and went docilely when they led him
out. The three of them walked past good cottonland laying fallow until they got to some old bottomland that
never did grow much of anything except rocks so big
they always had to plow around them. A crooked line
had always offended his daddy. His daddy believed in a
straight row of cotton. "A straight row of cotton is a sign
that a man take pride in his work boy. A man don't take
pride in his work ain't a man to do business with."

Bodeen was looking at the rocky field, crisscrossed
with haphazard but perfectly straight rows. A plow sat
at the head of the field like some guardian angel. It was
like he didn't want to understand, even when his daddy
started hooking up Booker T. Awareness began dawning
on him, but he fought it away. O daddy.

"Daddy," he said, "Daddy, this ain't no cottonland."

"Ain't got time for no foolishness boy. You don't
wanna work the cotton, ok, but don't get in my way."

He struggled with the harness.

"I'll help you daddy."

"Been thinking about letting you take the plow, you probably man enough now, what you think?"

His daddy hadn't let him take the plow until long after other boys his age were doing it. And when he did let his son plow, he walked alongside of him that whole season, watching and giving advice. Lucas took up the plow, his face twisting into a sad little smile when his daddy came up alongside him.

"Okay now boy pay me some attention now. One day this will all be yourn and you got to learn what it means to be a good farmer. Otherwise the land will beat you boy, it'll beat you down and leave you with nothing. You listening?"

"I'm listening daddy." He snapped the reins, wanting to do anything other than keep listening to his daddy talking nonsense, "Hee up now Booker."

Luke's row was the only crooked one in the whole field. Hadn't got but partway down his row before he was all sweated out and gasping for breath. Beside him his daddy struggled to keep up, but whenever Bodeen tried to stop or slow down he got a lecture on appropriate acreage. "Man with a good mule should be able to turn three, four acres a day boy. Get you a pace and hold it, thats what a good farmer does. Now, when you want to turn your ground for your crop?"

"Around the first of the year daddy."

His daddy smiled. "Might make a decent farmer out of you after all boy."

Bodeen felt a little warm glow in spite of himself. His old man had always been the best farmer in these parts, a serious man accumulating land in a county where coloredfolks wasn't allowed to get but so far ahead. In his prime he and Booker T could pull a cash crop out of land that wouldn't grow rocks. When neither him nor Mart took to farming, it liketa broke his daddy's heart. Everybody in West Tennessee knew he had hoped to find in his sons the love for the land that he had, but he never forced it on them. Too much the man to do that to his boys.

His daddy bent down and took up a handful of dirt, let it flow through his fingers and spread into the wind. "First year me and your momma came here this land was all rocks and trees. We had to clean it before we could plant it, me and her both. We didn't get but about two bales of cotton off this land that year. Second year we tamed it, got four fat, clean bales. Best year we ever had. Got more bales later, but that was the good one, that was the one that counted."

That evening Lucas Bodeen was whipped and they walked home slowly. His daddy was pleased with him. "Learn you good farming," he told Lucas proudly, "and you'll never go hungry. Get your own land and you'll never have to beg. Ain't no son of mine ever gon have to beg. You did good today son. I'ma make a farmer out of you yet."

Lucas turned his head away so that his daddy wouldn't see him cry.

"Thats all we got left," his momma told him that evening, his daddy asleep out back. "Sold most of the land and renting out the rest. Thats what we been living off of since your daddy's second stroke."

"Sold it, you sold the farm?"

Bodeen land.

"Ain't nobody to work it," she said. He was sorry he had brought it up. His old man had wanted so bad for his two boys to go into the farm with him. Luke Jr. hated the farm and farming and went on the road as soon as he was old enough to know how. At least Mart stayed till he turned a man before he went to Chicago.

That night Bodeen tore the house apart looking for liquor. Didn't find any. Probably best. He went to bed sober and unhappy. Dreamed he was back in that rocky field, plowing an eternal row of straight cotton behind Booker T, his daddy huffing and puffing beside him. Booker T started running away with him, and his daddy was trying to keep up, begging him to keep a straight row. Him and his daddy were both huffing and puffing and tugging on that plow when suddenly Bodeen was awake, lying on the cot in the kitchen wondering if he was dreaming still because he still heard the huffing and puffing. He was trying to shake off the confusion when his daddy shuffled into the room with the smallest of steps, his feet barely whispering on the floor. He shuffled on past Lucas into the front room, huffing and puffing like he couldn't get his breath to save his life.

"Daddy?" Lucas whispered so low he barely heard himself.

"Daddy." Lucas got up and went to him. "Daddy, you all right?"

His daddy didn't respond. He was scared to touch him, so he just stood there, wondering if it was okay to panic, when suddenly his momma was beside him, a thick robe pulled tight like she was cold in spite of the warmth of the night.

"He does that everynight that he can," she said. "It hard for me to sleep until he's through."

His daddy reached the front door, turned and started shuffling back at them.

"What's wrong?" He hesitated and added reluctantly, "With him."

She didn't answer for awhile. "He's fighting with death," she said finally. "He ain't ready to go and he just don't know how to die. You go back to sleep. I'll watch over him. I'm used to it."

Back on the cot in the front room, he laid there listening to his daddy's shuffling steps and labored breath. He turned his face to the wall when his daddy shuffled through the kitchen. It was bad enough listening, he didn't want to see it. He wanted only to see the man he remembered, big and strong and forever, daddy. He didn't hardly ever remember his daddy being sick, couldn't afford to be sick. Life sure was hard. His folks had worked hard all their lives and they were still struggling. Look like it don't ever let up on you, you just struggle on up to the day you die. When do you get to rest? He thought about how he been out here having a goodtime and using up his life in the fast lane while his family been back here struggling. They had always left him alone to do his thing. They had never called on him, never burdened him. Daddy had carried the weight as long as he could; his momma was carrying it now. One day it would be his turn. Just how serious a man would he be? Bodeen felt trapped. His momma

and his daddy needed rest. He couldn't leave them like
this.

Wasn't enough money coming in. The truck garden and
rent from folk as strapped as they were just wasn't getting it. Bodeen would have to go on the road to make
some real money but didn't feel like he could leave as
long as his daddy was determined to plow that rocky
field.

Him and his momma tried to make it easy on the old
man whenever they could. Every day it seemed he got
weaker and slower. And still every morning he could he
went out whether Lucas was ready or not. Bodeen got
so that he couldn't stand to see that redflannel workshirt,
his old man killing himself plowing dead land.

"We got to do something momma. He can't last much
longer like this."

"Can't stop your daddy from doing what he want
to do."

"I can try. He gon work himself into the grave
momma."

She nodded her head without conviction, too used to
daddy having his way. When his daddy came out that
morning, plaid working shirt buttoned wrong, Bodeen
stopped him. "Daddy, don't worry about going out today,
I'll do it."

"Do it?"

"I'll work the farm for you daddy, just like you taught
me. You got to rest. Daddy I'll do it. . . . Please."

His daddy looked at Lucas with tired eyes that

seemed to see all the times Lucas let him down. All the times Lucas didn't do what he said he'd do.

"I'll do it daddy. I'll do it all. You ain't got to do it no more. I plan to stay and I'll make sure that everything that got to get done get done. Just like you taught me, I swear it."

His momma smiled indulgently; she didn't believe him either.

"No, I will, I want to do it, I'm gonna do it. Please daddy."

"Lucas." His momma let her hand fall on his daddy's forearm. "He's right."

His daddy looked at him warily. Wanting to believe. How many times had he let his daddy down? Couldn't blame him for not believing him. Or in him. He brushed at the damp corner of his eye. "I'll do it daddy, I swear. You've done so much and I owe you so much daddy. If you don't take care of yourself, you gon be leaving us soon and then what will we do?"

His daddy was just sitting there, moving like he always did, slow and glacially ponderous. When he set his mind he was unmovable. The same power that had got him this far now turned against him.

"Daddy," said Bodeen finally, "ain't no cotton, ain't nothing but rocks out there. You plowing dead land daddy, its over."

His daddy grunted angrily and Lucas sat back. It was like he had just heard the warning cough of a toothless old lion. The king of the jungle's last roar in defense of the pride. The man he knew was still somewhere in that burnt-out husk. His daddy smiled a smile that wasn't a

smile, and was for a moment the grand old rock he had
always been. "Ain't no sense in you going out there
working land that ain't there," he said.

And then it was like he was suddenly shrunken,
smaller even as Bodeen sat there watching him. His
daddy seemed so suddenly lessened that Bodeen felt a
stab of guilt. But his daddy couldn't keep on working
like he was. It was clearly killing him. Lucas Bodeen
hugged his daddy carefully. "We still here daddy, thats
what counts."

Something went out of his daddy that morning. He'd get
up in the morning and go to sit on the front porch, and
he would stay there until it was time to go to bed. Never
a communicative man by nature, when he did speak,
spoke so slow and measured that you couldn't help but
try to help him get it out. But he didn't have anything at
all to say after he stopped working the land. He would
respond to you: you tell him its time to go to bed, he'd
get up and go, you tell him its time to eat he'd eat, but
he didn't speak. Through the day, he would keep turning
his chair to the sun, scrunching it around on the porch
so that the light would fall on his face as it moved
through the sky. He still walked the night. Momma put
her foot down when Lucas asked about it. "No," she said,
"leave him be."

With his time freed up, Bodeen visited his kinfolk.
Had Bodeens down Foster way and over on Royal Oaks.
He hunted down the same cronies he always saw when-
ever he was in town. Nan grows well. Boykin the King-

fish was scheming. Donwedward cussed him out for the
hell of it. Barbara made him smile. Found Gerald and
Safranski, Pume and Lisa playing dropdead poker, just
like the last time he was there, probably same game.

Found Dannyboy playing piano down at the local
juke. Joyce singing. One of the Dukes girls. They weren't
hardly through before he was up there hugging and
gladhanding. "Joyce. Dannyboy."

Joyce hugged him close, pretty little chipmunk face
full of smile. "Where have you been Lucas Bodeen?
Where you coming from now?"

He had to laugh; Joyce and Danny had a wanderfoot
as big as his. He had run up on both of them as far away
as Chicago or New York and never was surprised.

"Hey man," said Danny without missing a chord,
"how long you been in town?"

"Couple of weeks. Not long."

"How long you gon be here?"

"Don't know man, a family thing."

Dannyboy nodded. "Yeah, I go by occasionally, see
how they doing. Luann and Martin in town?"

"Naw, I'm the only one here."

"Hows your daddy?" asked Joyce.

"He could stand improvement."

"You ain't in to stay are you man? You know better."
Dannyboy shook his head while continuing to play; he
sounded bitter, his chords hard. "You stay around here
man you gon lose your touch. Ain't no jobs round here
for a musicman lessen you plan to chop cotton. Hey,
learn anything interesting in the last couple of years,
show us something."

He got up from the piano. Bodeen hesitated. Dannyboy caught the tic and pretty much pushed him down on the rickety wooden piano stool. Bodeen sat at the piano and stretched his fingers. He wanted a drink and started to order one. He stalled.

Truth be known, he was scared. Hadn't played the blues since he quit drinking, and was half afraid of what he'd hear when he sat down and tried to play straight. Been high since he learned how to play. Then too, he just didn't feel like the man he used to be. Had been forced to look inside and had found weakness where he thought only strength lay. Would rather plow dead land than find out he couldn't play a good blues no more.

But everybody was waiting on him, so he took a deep breath and played some tentative chords, cold dead licks. They could tell he was struggling with it. Then Joyce put a note on it for him, a high warbling note that filled the juke. One note of a whole song. He answered her almost instinctively with a walking bass. She came back with a lyric riff, and before you know it they were playing the blues. The crowd yelled appreciation, and a happy Bodeen played all night long.

"So when you coming by the house man," Danny asked before he left, "my wife gon be upset with both of us if you don't."

Went by Dannyboy's that weekend. Bodeen spent the whole evening envying. Family. The girls kept after him to tell stories they didn't no more believe than the man in the moon, fanciful tales of Carnival in Brazil and the talking drums of Africa. Of a magical city on the Nile named after Memphis Tennessee. About traveling up and down the river.

He stayed late. Warm and toasty and filled with bittersweet regrets. Life mighta been different, he thought, sweeter maybe, if I had stayed at home. If I had gone ahead and chose me a mate instead of chasing these blues like I done. He thought about how hard it would have been on his daddy now if he had been a man alone. He thought then of the women who had touched his life. Crystal images fine lifebright memories. Sha'ron. Bev. Lizbeth. The memories bought a warm satisfaction, and he sat there smiling to himself one of those special smiles. Brenda. Joyce. Robin. My Melvira. God, the women I have loved. Boy you been such a fool in your life.

I don't want to grow old alone.

"Melvira."

He heard himself before he realized he had said it. The faintest whisper, easily denied. Thoroughly disgusted with himself, he thrust the thought away, denied the soft warm feelings it unleashed. Don't want her on my mind or my heart. Next time Dannyboy invited him over he passed. No thanks.

Lucas came out the porch on his way over to the Foster Bodeens. His father sat in the chair facing the sun. "Hey daddy, you all right?" Not really expecting an answer, he was down the steps when his daddy spoke. "You in a hurry boy?"

"Uh, no daddy, I guess not."

"Sit down."

Lucas sat down on the top step, pleased that his daddy had asked him to. Even before his daddy took to the porch, he and his daddy rarely spoke beyond basics. Theirs was a quiet love. He sat on the porch and waited. His daddy didn't seem to have anything in mind but his company. At first he was uncomfortable, but the longer he sat the more the quiet evening got to him, and he started talking just to be talking and before he realized it, it just all came out of him, things he been wanting to say to his daddy for so long now. "You know daddy, I've always wanted to tell you how proud I am to be your son."

And like dawn breaking through the night he told his daddy who he was, told him how he felt about the blues, told him about Melvira and how bad it hurt him to lose her, even told him about going down. "I'm sorry daddy. I wasn't the man you taught me to be. I let you down."

His daddy didn't say much, just enough grunts and nods to keep him going, to indicate that he understood. He talked on long after the sun had moved in the sky. He so wanted his daddy to know who he was before it was too late. He was still talking when his daddy fell asleep. Without waking him, Lucas scooted his chair around to face the sun and covered him with a patchwork quilt that had been in his momma's family for generations. He kissed his daddy's hollowed-out cheek. "I love you so much daddy. All I've ever wanted to be was a man you could be proud of."

Dannyboy was right: wasn't much of a living to be had. Now that he was playing the blues again, he was anxious to play them. He started roaming further and further afield, wherever he could make a few dollars. First he just spend a couple of days gone at a time, then the days became weeks, old habits die hard. The last stubborn leaves of Autumn were falling from bare trees when he came home one Tuesday evening after playing down in Mound Bayou. In the face of a breezy northern wind he jumped down off a slow moving freight and started walking down the hill. He was feeling pretty good, had some folding money in his pocket, and had been hearing a new sound struggling to be born in his work. But when he crested the hill he saw a yard full of almost motionless people in somber suits and long dark dresses and he fell to his knees and cried, I swear to you daddy, I'm gon be a serious man, I swear it.

Luann came up to stay with momma and help out with the funeral arrangements. Was already there when Bodeen came down the hill that Tuesday Autumn evening. Martin couldn't make it from Chicago. Sent momma a telegram that she carried with her during the entire funeral. The funeral got loud and rowdy as good funerals tend to do, and it wasn't until the last festive straggler left that they had to face the strange quiet of daddy's absence. Elder Bodeen sat serenely amongst the mess, she who never allowed it. Luann started cleaning up.

"Don't bother," she said.

A little confused, Luann sat back at the table. "So what you gon do now momma," asked Luann, a hard, no-nonsense woman capable of facing life without the illusions that make it bearable for the rest of us. "You staying here or moving down with me and Jason?"

Momma went to the porch and looked into a sun setting on what used to be Bodeen land. "I'm catching the train to Chicago tonight," she said. "I've signed over what we got left to you and Jason. Do what you want with it. What you don't want sell. Lucas, I'm expecting you to take me to the train station. I be ready to go in about a hour."

"You gon leave the farm?"

Elder Bodeen ran her hand down curtains she had made, walked over a floor daddy had built and took down a large traveling bag already packed. "I'm leaving and I'm leaving tonight," she said with a bitterness that they had never before heard in her. "I've waited a long time to be able to leave here. Only reason that I stayed was cause your daddy loved it so. It took everything he had to give and then it took his life. I ain't got nothing else to give it. Not one more day."

Like a line of black warrior ants, a dust plumed caravan of old rattletrap cars followed an even more rattletrap flatbed truck down a dusty delta road. They pulled into a sleepy little Mississippi hamlet, left the flatbed at one end of town and musicians and pitchmen gathered at the other end. Horns blaring, they began cakewalking through town, telling corny jokes and calling out to folks, gathering a festive line of townfolk behind them. By the time they got back to the flatbed truck they had a nice-size crowd. Bodeen was already sweating when he sat down at his piano stool and started ragtiming. Doc Benson's Traveling Medicine Show. Step on up here yall. Let me tell you about Doc Benson's Medicational Elixir. For whatever ails you. Only 25 cents a bottle, 5 for a dollar.

Bodeen traveled with them for about four months and when he left, he left them riding in one of those old T-Models he won in a all-night coon can session outside of Tuscaloosa. Boy used that old T-Model Ford to ride all over the delta, never staying nowhere long, doing a little some of everything, from minstrel shows to weddings to country hoedowns to houseparties for a dollar a night and a redpop. Played jazz in a New Orleans bawdy house with high yella fancys dancing on his piano top and putting five-dollar bills in his shirtsleeve garter. Played the upstairs room at the Panama in Chicago, 40 dollars a week, top drawer in those days. Met a good woman on Fannin Street but she wasn't Melvira, and when he left her he wondered if he would ever love again. Or even if he wanted to. Heard one of his own songs once. In a pineywoods logging camp down in kneedeep Louisiana swamp.

I been born in real hard times,
roads been long and hard . . .

Stayed in the pineywoods camp till all the trees were gone and the land bare. The camp moved on and so did Bodeen. Played washboard bass when he couldn't find no piano. Pampered that old T-model from one end of the delta to the other. Everywhere but Beale. Drove through once or twice, always a weekend night, town closed down, no reason to stay. Don't think he would have ever gone back to Beale had it not been for Phineas T. Stokes.

been a long hard run
but I had my fun
I dared to be me.

The Larsens from down Indianola way never had any problems with their five stairsteps kids until they got to Memphis and their 15-year-old bucktoothed baby didn't come home for near on to three weeks. They searched until they found her in one of the Monroe Street cathouses, buried under layers of makeup and laughing in the arms of a slickhaired fancy man. Both of the roisterers were thoroughly entertained by the old couple's tearful pleas and countrified ways. A few discreet inquiries identified the pimp as St. Louis Slick. They took the name to Melvira Dupree.

"Hurt him hoodoo woman, hurt him bad."

She spoke for both of them, two tired old coloredfolks, rough thick veined hands entwined, sad yellowed eyes angry. The old man nodded a grim, silent agreement.

"St. Louie Slick Miz Melvira. A lowlife pimp and gambling man. Hurt him before he hurt our baby."

The pimps of Beale Street hung out over at Jacobs & Brownlee's barbershop when they weren't working. Nose wrinkling from the scent of sweet lotions and frying hair, Melvira found him there. He was sitting in a barbers chair getting his head conked, white barbers apron tied around his neck. From beneath the apron peeped pinstripe trousers and long narrow Stacey Adams shoes. He was a narrow-faced caramel-colored man with hooded eyes and smooth pampered skin. A young woman, in truth just a girl, stood next to him. A cultured veteran of Storyville, he watched Melvira approach him with a smooth professional interest.

"St. Louie Slick?"

Slick stared impassively from behind silvered shades. He saw a good-looking woman with a opennecked jar in one hand and a cork in the other.

He smiled his professional approval. "Yeah baby, thats me, what can I do for a fine young thing like you?"

Melvira corked the jar as soon as he answered her and walked out of the barbershop.

"What the hell is going on here?"

The overgrown little girl who had been sitting next to him nervously ran her tongue over her protruding front teeth and stood.

"Now where you going?" asked Slick.

"Your soul just got took Slick. I . . . I don't want to be around you when the hoodoo hit you."

Slick laughed it off. "Hoodoo? Who, me? Woman, I ain't got no soul. And that gal that just left here, she too damn fine to be no hoodoo."

That night candles flickered at the four corners of the earth and Melvira Dupree stared at a corked wide-necked jar. A curiously stained and murky jar. She was working but she lacked balance. She was bothered by what she did and the spell suffered. Yet to cut out the tribal poisons was her job. How many other healthy young souls had fallen into Slick's web? This enemy of the tribe. A justified hurting had never bothered her before the Hootowl filled her head with all this talk of her responsibility. She held the bottle up to the flickering candlelight and her nostrils flared. She would accept the stain on her soul. She did him in.

Wasn't too long before Lady Luck turned on ole Slick. First the cards stopped falling for him, he couldn't win fair or foul. Then there was this string of accidents, busted an ankle, broke a rib, accidentally cut himself, 12 stitches. Caught the crabs from one of his women and took them home to his wife, and his girlfriend. Then he got stabbed by some hick who accused him of cheating in a poker game where everybody was cheating but the hick. Ripped up his best suit doing it too. Boy's mind started wandering on him, couldn't keep his concentration for worrying so. And the voices. His stable left him. Before you knew it he was down and out. Living in the street. Coughing blood. Cursing the full moon. Got so bad folks started calling him by his real name, Pompey. Those that took the time to call him at all.

Yet candles still flicker at the four corners of the earth and an uneasy conjure woman walks the early morning riverbluff. She seeks a sign. The Work had been so much easier back in Sweetwater. Was this worthy of a child of Oluddumare? What did she have for her people if not magic? And what of the Larsens, her clients? Does this truly solve their problem? Does she nurture strength or spread weakness where weakness already reigns? Blackfolk so often bring to the hoodoo problems they do better to struggle with. The way of life is one of struggle. Where was the service here?

Just then, as it often does, the morning sun turned the muddy river to gold. She stopped, awed and enthralled, one with the unspeakable beauty of nature. As much a part of that nature as a rock or a tree. The sky or the ocean. The universe. True, she had things to do, problems to meet, but there is always time to enjoy God and the pleasure of cosmic harmony. Is this her sign? Was not all that happens in life the voice of God?

Oluddumare mojuba

It would be far more rewarding here, she thought as she bathed in the river's gold, to feed souls rather than destroy one. To give the Larsens the strength of soul that would enable them to meet this challenge and any other. The power to extract strength from adversity and pleasure from struggle. To live and grow well. So—she gave the Larsens, all three of them, Highjohnny Conquer root and instruction in the way of things. As for Slick, she let him go. Upon realizing that his soul was his own again, Slick decided that he had felt the cool breath of God. Gave up his wild and wooly ways and took up preaching. Became an itinerant delta holyman of considerable spiritual prowess. Had a knack for souls.

Increase in harmony.

Good fortune.

Good hoodoo.

The night so bristled with stars that the river glowed. On the bluff an easy riverbreeze danced with her night-white shawls. Below, the Hootowl's Roost bumped against the cobblestones the foot of Beale. She hesitated. Somehow she knew that this was a door that once opened would not be closed. Downriver an anxious old catfish slapped water and the conchhorn calls. Gather together. She sighed and walked on down to the driftwood houseboat tied to at the foot of Beale

"Why me?" is her question. "I don't want this burden."

The Hootowl shrugged, "Who knows the whys of Oluddumares Plan. All I know is that this ground is holyground. I been noted for awhile now Miz Dupree that the hoodoo way got to be something more than what it is. I ain't the one. I think you are."

"And what if I wont?"

He shrugged sympathetically. They both knew she had no choice. She had been hit with the Hoodoo Curse, the vision to see what must be done and the knowledge that you are capable of doing it. Fate does offer choices of a sort. There are many destinies and it is in the choosing that humanity is at its best. But some choices are Fa, the choice that is not a choice. Fate is God's idea of fun and games.

"You will," said the Hootowl. "My constant study Miz Dupree is people, to know you when you walk through my door better than you know yourself. I seen you watching the coloredfolks coming in out of the delta and I seen you concerned. I know you see what I see, and I know you realize that they are our responsibility. Always have been. Just like you took care of your folks back in Sweetwater you got to do for the race. And for all God's creatures great and small. We been a weak people, we been a weak way, but thats going to change. And I say its going to be on you. I say that the ground you walk on will be holyground." He chuckled, his everpresent amusement at life's tricks bubbling free. "Specially if you continue to listen to my teachings like you doing now. Oh I got a few magic tricks to show you, too, magic is a handy tool, but a hoodoo that don't go past magic don't really understand the hoodoo way. The primacy of the sorcerer is past," said the Hootowl. "We must now walk the way of the prophet."

Firstborn
Your way has been hard
and harder still
for in you I have purpose
In you I have a plan.
Listen well
and you
shall be
close to
God

It was early one Sunday in a little cornerhole jook outside of Itta Bena. The sun rose on three leftovers from the night before: Swampdog, the owner of the place, Lucas Bodeen and a tired traveling man at a corner table. Bodeen had played all night. Swampdog had just paid him and he was just sitting at the piano playing some music in his head before getting on the road to

Senatobia. It was a good well-tuned piano and he liked playing it. Most of the jukejoint pianos he played were in bad shape and he was usually forced to play around dead keys. Had little calluses on his fingertips from playing pianos where the ivory was worn off the wood. The traveling man had sat through the night, too, told Swampdog he was waiting on the early morning train. A black bowler sat on the table in front of him and a blue carpetbag sat beside his booted foot. He fiddled with the same half-filled glass he had started the evening with. Swampdog, limping on his short left leg, walked around upending chairs on the tables until the room was filled with upturned spiders. He put away every chair but Lucas' and the traveling man's and began vigorously sweeping, obviously waiting for the two of them to leave.

"I got to be closing up soon," he muttered. "Got a wife waiting at home you know."

Bodeen was bent over the piano keys as if he hadn't heard. The traveling man seemed determined to sit as long as he could. Swampdog shrugged. He'd give them both till he was ready to mop. Actually he was feeling pretty good. He drew a couple of glasses of his private bootleg bonded whiskey. Prohibition had been declared but wasn't being enforced yet. He sat one in front of Bodeen and without looking up Bodeen shook his head, No thanks.

Embarrassed at the refusal of his generous impulse, Swampdog snapped at Bodeen, "Bout time for me to close up," and started sweeping again. Bodeen ignored him.

Deep in a bittersweet melancholy, Bodeen let his hands wander over the keyboard, waiting for the spirit to move him. He had been thinking about Melvira, missing her for the first time in awhile now, thinking about life without her. He was half pissed cause he had thought he was over her. Wished he had never met her. He had been self-sufficient before, didn't need nothing or nobody. Now he knew something was missing in his life. A hole even the blues don't fill. O Melvira. O baby. I miss you so. He let missing her flow through his fingers. You could hear it in his every note. O baby, I miss you so. His music became more mood than melody, and he felt all the pain he'd been carrying swelling in him. A piece about Melvira began to grow. A meditation on love.

Swampdog put his broom down, pulled one of the chairs down from the top of a table and sat down to listen.

I've come a long long way
to get to where I am.
I've walked naked
through the fire and the storm.

Lucas Bodeen let the music say all the things he wanted to say to her. O baby, I love you so. I don't understand why or nothing, I just love you. Lucas Bodeen played his heart out, another man hurting cause my baby's gone and o the loving sure was good blues.

O God baby, how could you really leave me?

Tears.

His own eyes misty, Swampdog limped to the door and stepped out onto the porch. Some things you just don't watch a man go through if you want to remain his friend. Swampdog sat on the porch and watched the morning come. Lost in his own melancholy memories of good loving gone. The one. That special one. His weak eyes unfocused over painfully sweet memories.

And the one thing I've learned
is a good woman must be earned

After awhile the music start getting good to him, and ol Bodeen, he forgot all about how bad he felt. Got into the music, made that piano stand up and do tricks. No matter how much trouble you got in mind, the blues tend to remind you that the sun is going to shine in your back door someday. For all the pain it cost him, he had to say he was glad she had come into his life. Don't do for a man to live and die without having known at least one great love in his life. He would have hated to have died without having ever felt like she made him feel.

Outside, Swampdog smiled, nodding his head and patting his feet. Being a good old delta boy himself, Swampdog knew how to listen to the blues, and what he heard the new pace say is that you need to get out there early in life and find the woman that really moves you. She's out there, the one that you willing to die for. You court her and you get her and you hold on to her as if your life depended on it, growing as necessary to love her properly and well. Don't wait till you hit the wall, till all you got left is a story to tell and another good loving blues to sing.

Swampdog thought about the woman waiting at home for him. A good old gal for a good old boy. He was a lucky man to get another shot at love. Blessed. Listening to Bodeen's Blues caused the old Dog to decide right then and there that he was gon treat that woman of his real real good. Takes a fool to lose love twice, said Bodeen's Blues, only a fool is a fool all his life.

I'm man enough to keep you warm

The bowler-topped traveling man approached Bodeen. "Mr. Bodeen? Phineas T. Stokes at your service. Pleased to meet you. My distinct pleasure. You are Mr. Lucas Bodeen, correct?"

Still playing, Bodeen nodded that he was.

"Also known as Delta Luke Bodeen?"

A raised eyebrow conceded the point.

"I had heard of you Mr. Bodeen. I came here last night strictly to hear you play. You were good, but I wasn't sure. Fortunately for both of us, what I heard you do just now was genius. I'm a scout for Okeh records Mr. Bodeen and we'd like you to record for us. Pay you two thousand dollars cash money. What do you say?"

Bodeen stopped playing and looked at him. It was too sweet to be believed. A record deal. His work on record. Forever. Finally. Unwilling to trust his voice, he nodded and played a triumphant chord. Sure.

"Fine Mr. Bodeen, we'll arrange for a ticket to our studios in New York. Leaving out of Memphis, say a week from Sunday, have you back in two weeks, two thousand dollars and a couple of recordings richer. What do you say Mr. Bodeen?"

"I say why wait. I'll be there Sunday coming, ready to play."

"Splendid, I can see its going to be a pleasure working with you Mr. Bodeen. Look, heres a hundred advance. See you at the Illinois Central train station in Memphis, Sunday, say about twelve o'clock? Deal?"

They shook hands. Deal.

A timid knock on the door rose Melvira Dupree from her altar.

"Come in."

A thin holloweyed woman bent over a small blue bundle opened the door slowly. Her body knotted tight with a pain of the soul.

Melvira looked away. "I can't help you."

The woman started crying. "You don't know what I want."

"I know what you want. There's nothing I can do."

The holloweyed woman just stood there crying silently, paralyzed with the injustice of it all. Melvira took the little blue bundle from the shaking hands and unwrapped it: an infant child staring up at her with trusting eyes starbright with fever. A sick heat rose from the child, and Melvira dropped her eyes.

"I can't help you," she said again. She held out the baby, her own eyes now as sad as the hollowed ones.

"You got to save my baby," said the woman, refusing to take the tattered bundle back. "What good are you hoodoo woman?"

The smell of death was strong and bitter. The baby stared and the sadeyed woman waited.

"I cant help you," said Dupree. "Long past time I could do anything for her."

"I took her to the CME colored hospital, they said nothing they can do."

"Theres nothing I can do."

Melvira saw the desperation spring in the woman's eyes and didn't try to stop her when she turned and fled down the stairs. Her heart went out to the little brown child staring so silently up at her. Wasn't enough spirit left to pull back from the grave, but she tried anyway, placed the child to her naked breast and let the dry hot fever surge into her body. Death fever. More than she could ever assume. The slightest little tremor quickly supressed. Restless. She dressed, wrapped the blanket tight into her arms and hurried out into the night. She was walking down Beale toward Pontotoc when a little knot of Beale Street kids saw her and began following behind her.

"Hoodoo woman, hoodoo woman."

She ignored them, but they bothered her. Back home hoodoos had been treated with respect and even fear. Folks believed in them. Without belief there is no power. Without power there is no respect. When the children realized what she carried, they yelled even louder, more viciously. "Babykiller. Hoodoo babykiller." An elderly woman made the sign of the cross and stepped off the sidewalk to let her pass. Suddenly tired, Melvira Dupree turned and stared at them. They ran away, yelling over their shoulders, "Babykiller. Babykiller."

She continued down the almost deserted Beale, stiff and unyielding, practically unaware of everything around her. Till she felt him. She stopped and stared at a shadow standing in the darker shadows of a doorway. Her eyes became angry slits.

"Face me," she commanded.

The Baron stepped out of the shadows. He stood there patiently, hat in hand.

"This lacks dignity Miz Dupree. I'm just doing my job. Just like you."

He nodded politely, put his hat back on his head and stepped back into the darkness. The gods turn their backs. They o so often do.

She would not waste her appeal. She drew the bundle closer to her and walked with stiff purpose down Beale to Pontotoc. Red door, white house. 711. Doctor Flowers.

There were no lights and she who never cried felt the reluctant tracks of tears as she knocked on the door. A porchlight came on, throwing her elongated shadow into the darkness behind.

"Who in the hell is it?" an irritated voice inside muttered. "Its three in the morning dammit."

"Doctor." Her voice cracked. She composed herself. "Doctor, I have a sick child."

A pause. Then the sound of locks being snapped open. The door opened and old Doc Flowers stood there in a robe, crinkly gray hair fringed around a bald dome, peering at her nearsightedly. He recognized her. "O its you. One of them."

He started to close the door and she held the child out to him.

"Doctor."

He stopped and peered down at the bundle.

"She was brought to me about a half hour ago. There's nothing I can do for her. Your colored hospital says she's going to die. . . . So do I."

He looked at her first, then at the child in her arms, with that special look peculiar to their profession. No doctor likes losing a patient.

"Surprised you got sense to leave healing to the doctors, got more sense than most of your kind. Bring her in," he said, turning away from the door. Melvira just stood there, holding the baby in outstretched hands.

He realized she wasn't following and turned back to her. "Well come on, or do you plan to do more harm than you've assuredly already done? Come on now."

He took the bundle from her and walked away from the opened door toward a sitting room, yelling into the back, "Gwen, where's my bag?"

Melvira turned to leave.

"You!" he barked. "Aren't you going to help?"

"You do your job, I'll do mine."

She walked back to Hernando with her head down and her shoulders slumped. A phrase the Hootowl had used in his instruction came to her. "Tribal Guardian. Tribal Guide." She fixated on it, a light in the darkness. Just what was the role of the hoodoo way in the new world? The old ways no longer worked. Her lack of understanding plagued her as never before and she slept fitfully that night.

But that was the night that her traveling spirit moved with surety and purpose. A stream, a wooden bridge. Cross the bridge and follow a winding treelined path through a thick woods. A formation of crows wheel overhead and a ivy-covered cabin hides in a deep delta fog. A rooster scratches furiously at a dirtbare yard. She woke in a sweat, a name in her mind, whispered into the night. "Taproot. Taproot Mississippi."

Lucas Bodeen slowly drove down Main Street Memphis toward the Illinois Central train station. He was supposed to meet his cousin there and leave his car with him till he got back from New York. He was a little early so he got out to stretch his legs, leaning on the side of his car, watching the crowd pass and enjoying being back in Memphis after being too long gone. He wondered idly if Mel was still in town, rather pleased with himself that he had felt no urge to go see. Well boy, looks like you finally got her out your system. A big damned relief. And about to record his songs. Life was looking good for Luke Bodeen.

"Mr. Bodeen?"

He looked up. A well-dressed colored man stood before him, silk top hat in hand. The harsh lines of his face seemed softened somehow by the scars carved into his cheeks. When he smiled his gums were blue.

"Good evening Mr. Bodeen."

"What can I do for you my friend?"

"I come with information Mr. Bodeen, about a mutual friend of ours."

Oh hell thought Bodeen, the deal was off. Maybe it was just that his cousin couldn't make it. "Who from, Stokes or my cousin?"

"Neither Mr. Bodeen."

Bodeen frowned. "I don't know you do I? What instrument do you play?"

"Souls Mr. Bodeen, are my favorite instrument."

Bodeen grimaced. He had lived with a hoodoo too long not to recognize the style.

"I'm here regarding a Miss Melvira Dupree."

Damn. He had been doing so well.

"She's leaving town at this very moment Mr. Bodeen. She's walking down Main."

"Just who are you friend?"

"I am Mr. Bodeen a practitioner of the mystical sciences."

"And whats all this to you Mr. Practitioner of the Mystical Sciences? Did she send you?"

"We both know her better than that Mr. Bodeen."

Bodeen's smile had no humor to it. "Yeah, I guess we do don't we?"

And then he saw his cousin coming down the street. And he saw Phineas T. Stokes jump out of a cab and stride up to the train station looking around for him. They both saw him at about the same time and started toward him.

"Well its been nice talking to you Mr. Practitioner but I got a train to catch. I got some people eager to pay me to do what I've wanted most in my life to do."

"Quite right Mr. Bodeen," said the scarred man. "You strike me as a man who refuses to accept anything less than what he really wants out of life."

On
Traveling
Down
Dusty
Old
Delta
Roads

YEAR FOUR

Seems nobody ever heard of any Taproot Mississippi. The Illinois Central ticket agent delicately scratched at his balding head. "Sorry mam, never heard of it. Whats it near? You sure its in Mississippi?"

She rode the almost empty trolley as far down Main as it took her and got off and started walking, traveling grip in hand. South. If her traveling spirit said Taproot Mississippi, then Taproot Mississippi it was. Trust the power. She hadn't walked very far when an old T-model Ford pulled up alongside of her. She looked up and sitting there grinning at her was Luke Bodeen, white bloused sleeve shirt, black string tie, derby hat wore cocked to the side, a red rose held crosswise in his teeth.

Wearing almost a smile, she stopped and stared up at him. He didn't say a word, looking at her through one of his cocky Bodeen grins. She tried to keep an answering quirk from her own lips. Felt good to know that he was still in there trying. A woman cant help but respond to that kind of devotion. She felt some of that old feeling stirring, felt his hard male desire reach out and lick her body. No. The ripple of excitement was not allowed to ripen. She would take no chances with a passion of the magnitude offered in Bodeen's hungry eyes.

Heart. Or body. Whichever. Listen. I am master here.

He climbed out of the Ford, took the rose from his teeth and offered it with a flourish. Now its hard to pull off a move like that without looking like a fool, you got to really believe. Bodeen was a believer. She took it.

"Nice day for a walk," he says. "Even nicer day for a ride in this here fine automobile."

This here fine automobile choose that moment to shimmy and fart a cloud of black exhaust smoke. My boy was cool, he didn't bat a eye. Melvira had to smile.

"And how you been Bodeen?"

He was listening for music, but the question was a statement not a song. He was disappointed but not surprised. She saw it.

"Lucas . . ." She started to rein him in.

"We wont," he said, holding up a cautioning finger, "even speak on the fact that you don't know where Taproot Mississippi is. I do. Two," he counted another finger, "why walk if you can ride? Three," another finger, "notice if you will."

He pointed. A picnic basket in the back of the automobile.

"Lovely day for a picnic, no?"

He reached into the backseat and pulled out a jug beaded with coldsweat. He turned it up and took a long drink, ignoring her frown. He took the jug down with a loud sigh and wiped his lips. He offered it to her.

"Water. Cold too. Good for you too. Keeps the system clean."

"Bodeen . . ." She laughed and she realized how long it had been since she laughed.

"Four," he held up a fourth finger, and pulled back a red blanket on the floor of the car. A Georgia ham. A great big green striped watermelon. He thumped it. A nice hollow thump.

"Ripe and juicy," he said, "just like you."

"Bodeen . . ."

"Okay then, back to my best point. What you gon do, walk to Taproot? Do you realize how far it is? Long way to Taproot Mississippi girl, specially seeing as you don't even know where it is."

She hated to ask. "How did you know I was looking for Taproot Mississippi?"

"I'ma bluesman baby, I know everything about life worth knowing, you know that."

"Unhuh," she said, waiting for a better answer.

"Little guy, thick set, old eyes," he said. "Smart dresser but somewhat out of style. Scars on his face."

"I don't suppose theres any chance of you just telling me how to get there." Her traitorous lips twitched again.

He shook his head. "None whatsoever. You can forget that."

She didn't know whether to be pleased or mad at him.

And then in a quicksilver moment he dropped the manmask of cool and stood naked before her. "Aw come on Mel. I just take you to Taproot and I wont bother you none on the way, least no more than you let me."

Didn't have to be a hoodoo to know he was lying through his teeth. But she wanted to go with him so she would. Him just showing up like this was surely a sign. Who was she to argue with the gods? Except when she wanted to. But she knew that devotion like Bodeen's carried a price.

"Bodeen, this doesn't change a thing. What we had is past and you just gon embarrass yourself for nothing. Then you gon be mad at me."

"I wouldn't exactly call you nothing Melvira Dupree. Problematic maybe, but not nothing."

"Taproot Mississippi Bodeen. Thats it, okay."

"Sure," he said, opening the door. A crooked straw broom fell out at her feet. He put it in the backseat and bowed her into the car with a smile. "Trust me."

They drove toward Mississippi in a fairly comfortable silence. It was Mel's first time in an automobile, and she was enjoying the experience, which pleased Bodeen, so they were both in a good mood. He kept looking at her out the corner of his eye. Being with her again had been a fantasy of his for so long that being with her for real felt strange. Another dream. When he had seen her walking down Beale like the hoodooman told him she would, it was like the world stopped. Just stopped dead still. Then it started again; his heart beat, the sun moved in the sky. His little side glances were hungry ones. She must have changed in four years. He had. He had gone through so many changes in the last couple of years he felt like a different man. Older, wiser maybe, definitely more raggedy around the edges. Far less sure of things than he once was. Melvira, she looked just like she did the day he left her.

The morning was quiet with few cars, wagons or people on the road. Once they left Memphis they had the world to themselves.

"Go ahead Bodeen."

"Go ahead?"

"Talk. Sing. Let those pretty words just roll on off your tongue." She laughed, head thrown back and offering the long line of her neck for his devotion.

He kept his eyes on the road. Far as he was concerned, being there said it all. "Guess I'm satisfied to leave well enough alone. Your momma in Taproot?"

"Yes."

"What else you learn about her?"

Melvira felt vaguely guilty. "Not much. My mind has been elsewhere."

"You been looking?"

"No. Not really."

He kept looking over at her as he drove, just unable to believe she was really there. He ached to touch her. To hold her. Instead he concentrated on his driving. Halfway pissed with himself. Cause he didn't really expect to win this one. When the scarred hoodoo made him look at himself, Bodeen had cursed him soundly. Cause he had to try.

By the time they hit 61 South they felt almost comfortable. Bodeen was just too satisfied to stay subdued for long. Life had point and purpose again. He savored the deltawind blowing through the car. The day was clear and the air was fresh and all you could see as far as you could see was pretty green delta country, just begging for a picnic. He started looking for suitable grounds.

"What are you looking for?"

"Someplace to have our picnic."

"Picnic?" Her voice lacked enthusiasm.

"Picnic, you know, picnic? Thats the price of my traveling services. When was the last time you went on a picnic?"

"Never been," she said almost proudly.

"Well Melvira Dupree look to me you got more to learn about life than you think. Keep a eye out for some pretty ground."

Her protests were weak and insincere. So they picnicked. Pretty sun, cool breezes, birds, butterflies and floating half notes. And she enjoyed herself. Enjoyed being with him. He was so much calmer than she remembered. Her senses twitched approvingly.

While feasting on red ripe watermelon they brought each other up to date on their lives, on who they were these days. Easy no hassle conversation. As usual Bodeen took liberties with the truth, but you couldna proved it by him. If you were to ask him he'da swore every word was true. And so it was. He resisted making his moves on her until the last minute. "So then I figured," he said while rolling up the blanket, "that it was time to come back and get you. Figured you might be ready by now."

"Bodeen."

"Well you know I'm gon try Melvira," he said with wide-eyed innocence. "Just tell me 'no.' I take a 'no' easy."

She laughed. She had always been susceptible to Bodeen at play. She felt like she hadn't laughed in years. Bodeen watched and wanted. Behind his casual good cheer, his throat is dry with need. Patience Bodeen. Like a flathead tom stalking a hot little pussycat. Calm, steady, unrelenting patience. Do you want her or don't you?

By the time they climbed back into the car they were old friends again, years stripped away like they had never been. They drove due south, Bodeen steady telling her not to worry, Taproot wasn't that far down the road. It was a nice warm delta day and the folk were out in force, so they did a lot of waving, at kids rolling hoops alongside the car, folk in fields and yards and sitting on porches. On the delta they partial to waving and greeting folk, to smiling and showing you their teeth. They drove past rolling delta hills and wide open fields, huge plantations and ramshackle shacks and little kids with thin arms and swollen bellies, who still yet waved and laughed and smiled and ran alongside the car for as long as they could. They made Melvira pensive, she saw an agony in the folk, in the poverty and the lack of spirit that she had not particularly noticed before. But at the same time she could see a strength hidden there, just waiting for the key to unlock it. Her lost beautiful people. Ole Bodeen, he was just happy, and he don't even see the downside of the delta. A getting-around man, he's seen a lot of ground in his day. But he always came back home, mostly cause of the folk, goodfolk, thick and solid and built to last. They move slow but they usually get where they going.

On this particular day, Lucas and Melvira hadn't got but so deep into Mississippi when Bodeen pulled over in front of a big old house with a wraparound porch. Elders sat on the porch fanning themselves with heart-shaped church fans on a stick and a gaggle of little brown kids washed their feet at the front yard pump. Leaving the car running, Bodeen got out and dusted himself off.

"Be right back baby," he said as he sauntered over to the porch and commenced a conversation full of pointing and head scratching on the part of the sitting elders. Melvira looked up. The sky was turning fiercely dark. Bodeen came back over and climbed in the drivers seat, ignoring her eloquently arched eyebrow.

"Nice folks," he said.

"What was that about Bodeen?"

"Oh nothing much, mostly asking instruction on how to get to Taproot."

"I thought you knew how to get to Taproot Bodeen."

He pulled out into the road. "So I lied."

They were driving down a little winding road when they entered a vast cottonfield, furry white acres stretching the horizon. Leaving a trail of dust behind them, they drove through the big cottonfield slowly, fascinated with the white fluffy expanse of it. They come to a dusty little delta crossroads in the middle of the field when old faithful spluttered, shimmeyed and stopped.

Bodeen just sat there in a state of shock. Had driven her all around the country without no problem. And she chose right now to stop on him. Why you do me like this baby? Cursing like a bluesman, Bodeen climbed down and went under the hood. After awhile and he hadn't come out, Melvira joined him.

"Whats wrong?"

"Don't work," he muttered.

"Very good Bodeen."

"I just drive em."

Melvira looked up at the sky with concern. "We better get inside. Its going to rain. Heavy."

And the skies opened and the rains came.

Nathaniel Bland's family had been living up against the river now for four generations. He himself had grown up alongside the river, every house they ever had was built up on little brickhigh water pilings. He had told Ollie Mae before they got married that he could tell when the river was rising by his game leg. His riverleg he called it. And proved it too during the floods of 1912,

'13 and '17, when he warned folk the river was coming long before it got there. So they paid heed when he woke up one morning clutching his bad leg. "Rivers rising," he said, "gon be bad this time." Hard words in the delta, "rivers rising." River he was referring to, of course, the Mississippi. The Big Muddy. As common to mighty rivers, it served as a major artery for the continent. Towns and cities flourished on its banks, and it covered the land it bordered with a black soil so rich a good crop liable to just spring out the ground for you. Deltafolk consider Old Man River a personal friend. But every once in a while he liable to turn on you. Nat's neighbors had cause to be concerned. Last time, the big flood of 1917, they found Mrs. Solomon's boy drowned three miles deep into Arkansas. Lost six folk and most every building in town.

Mrs. Chase called her cousin up in Missouri. "Sure enough, its raining heavy up that way," she told Nat. "They got people out working on the levees above St. Joe already."

May June Clarabell's boy from over in Memphis called and said that the Sheriff's Department was going down Beale rounding up the coloreds. Said he had been waiting to see a movie over at the New Daisy and they pulled him out of the line in his suitcoat, made him leave his wife and children there and put him to work on the levee. Said he had just got away and called to warn that the river rising. But all this was just confirmation. They trusted Old Man Bland's riverleg more than they trusted the Memphis Sheriff's department. They immediately commence to moving to high ground.

The rains was unreal. Soaking wet Bodeen climbed back in the car. The rain beat a tattoo against the roof of the car. The four spokes of their crossroads disappeared into the raining darkness, and the world closed in on them. They hadn't been there long before a shape appeared in the rain-misted south spoke of the crossroad. A shape vague and silent and muffled by the heavy rains. As it got closer they saw that it was a big ancient wagon pulled by a huge plodding black mule. The wagon stopped. Sat. Directly, a smaller shape separated itself from the wagon and walked toward them. Closer they see a grizzled old blackman, eyes hidden under an old slouch hat that sluiced off the rain and an equally old shotgun cradled in his arms. Melvira tried to look beyond the surface and was met with a blank wall of power.

Bodeen jumped down into the muddy track of the crossroads. "How do cousin? You know anything about these here automobiles, or maybe where we can get one fixed?"

The old guy nodded. Slowly, deliberately, all the time in the world.

Bodeen waited for clarification. It wasn't coming.

"Yes you know where we can get it fixed," he asked impatiently, "or yes you know how to fix it?" His only answer was the bob of the slouch hat in the darkness. Now Bodeen is getting a attitude. Caught in the rain. His trusty little car broke. Tramping across the delta looking for some place don't nobody know of with a woman that don't wanna be with him.

"You haven't even looked at it friend. You don't even know whats wrong with it."

Melvira came down, put a calming hand on his arm and stepped in front of him. "We'd be much obliged," she said to the old man, "if you can help us. Can you fix it?"

The old man nodded, the movement of the slouch hat again throwing off water.

"Will you?"

The old man nodded again and went back to his wagon, flesh become shadow until he disappeared into thicker shadow. The rain muffled all sound. Bodeen goosebumped.

"Talkative old cuss ain't he?" Bodeen muttered. He looked at Melvira suspiciously. He had been with her long enough to recognize that uncomfortable twinge of the spirit world brushing ours.

The old man came back to them with a chain in one hand, shotgun still in the other. Without putting the shotgun down, he and Bodeen hooked the car up to the wagon. Bodeen restrained his customary irreverence. Motioning Bodeen back in the car, the old man once again disappeared behind the veil of rain. They sat in quiet anticipation till with a jerk the car started forward. Bodeen kept looking at Melvira while they crawled along behind the wagon, but he didn't say anything. If it was a hoodoo thing, he didn't really want to know. All he knew was that he was with his baby again, and a wise man expects thorns with his roses.

Rivulets of water had found their way in before they finally pulled up before a small farmhouse perched on brick highwater pilings. A comfortable little spread with a ramshackle barn to the side. The old man pulled up in front of the barn.

"This it cousin?" Bodeen yelled above the rain.

The old man nodded. Bodeen climbed down and worked the big double doors while the old man unhooked the car. Then they pushed it inside the barn.

Melvira unhitched the mule and brought it in.

"Thanks for getting us out of that water cousin. This where you gon fix me up?"

Without reply the old man began rubbing down the big black mule, shotgun now slung from his back with a string. Bodeen turned Melvira a questioning eyebrow. The old man jerked his thumb at the house.

"Sure you don't need any help here cousin?" asked Bodeen, reluctant to leave his precious automobile with this funny acting old guy. The old man jerked his thumb again, and Melvira led Bodeen to the door.

"Come on Bodeen," she said, "let him work."

They stood at the door, getting up their nerve to go dashing out into the rain. A door opened in the house and a little petite woman stood there waving them over. Two kids peeped from behind a long groundsweeping skirt. Bodeen and Melvira sprinted through the rain and darted inside, soaking wet.

Half expecting her to be strange as the other guy, Bodeen started explaining immediately. "We came in with the old man. I think he's fixing our automobile. Wouldn't swear to it though. Wasn't exactly a friendly fella."

She beamed. "Oh don't yall worry about him, he just not inclined to say no more than he have to."

She shooed em in like she had been waiting on them, a little woman, with a warm little sincere smile like a lighthouse in a fog. "Yall take off those wet clothes now. Here, put these on."

She handed them a handful of dry clothes. Everytime she moved, the two little kids peeping around her skirt moved so that she was between them and the newfolk. The place was dry and homey, the rain pittypattering the roof. They were immediately comfortable. An old woman sat in a rocking chair beside the fire, looking at them from coalpit eyes.

"Momma Gerri," said the petite woman. The old woman nodded and turned back to the fire, using a stick to stir the embers. A rough carved bowl sat beside her. Melvira noticed that it had seven High John de Conquer roots in it.

"And I'm Ella. Yall mighty welcome, and just in time for dinner. We thank you for the blessing." She pulled the two kids out from behind her skirt. "This here is Sista, and this one here is Bubba."

The little girl and boy stared at them with wide-eyed wonder.

"Which one are you now?" Melvira asked the little girl.

"I'm Sista."

"And I'm Bubba."

"Yall married?" Sista asked Melvira.

Bodeen laughed. "Sho we married, ain't we married Melvira?"

"Yall kids let em change now," said Ella, "don't bother em till they comfortable. You know better."

They darted back behind their momma's skirt, and

she pointed Luke and Melvira at a little room with a
blanket cutting it off from the rest of the house. Once
in the room, Luke and Melvira began shucking out of
their wet clothes. At least Melvira did. Bodeen watched,
admiring the way the wet material clung to the fleshy
parts of her body. She impatiently motioned for him to
turn around. He refused. Why should I? She hissed at
him. He laughed and turned and began dressing in the
humongous overalls Ella had given him.

"Who this tent belong to?" he asked when he came
out looking like a clown, the straps tied up around his
shoulders and a rope around his voluminous middle.

"Junior. My honey."

"Junior? A junior what?"

"You. Girl. Come here."

The old woman by the fire. The wooden bowl was
now in her lap and her hand handled the seven roots
inside. She motioned for Melvira to sit beside her. The
minute she sat, Sista darted over, determined to be included in anything that involved this strange beautiful
woman who had come out of the delta rain, this woman
who must be one of those great and magical women of
Guinee that Momma Gerri told of in her stories. Is
Nzinga Momma Gerri? Harriet Tubman? Sweet Georgia
Brown? Miz Grace? Patrice? Safiya? Who Momma Gerri?

Momma Gerri shushed Sista's avalanche of questions
before they came. "Shhh now chile, you ask her, she'll
tell you who she is."

Sista was too shy to do that, but she did go over and
crawl into Melvira's lap. Momma Gerri rocked, fingers
idly playing with the Conquer roots in her bowl. She

threw one of her roots into the fire and intently watched a little flame flare up and settle. She turned to Melvira. Melvira felt the featherbrush touch of her regard.

"What you looking for child?" she asked softly.

"Taproot Mississippi."

The woman nodded.

"Taproot a difficult place to find."

Handling the six roots left in the bowl, she seemed to forget all about Melvira.

"Don't you mind Momma Gerri," said Ella, while laying out a steaming plate of biscuits. "She like to mystify folks with that hoodoo talk."

When Melvira didn't answer, Ella smiled knowingly.

"Of course, if you understand her then don't mind me. Just go right on bout your business."

Melvira came over to help Ella set the table, losing herself in the small domestic chores. Then the door banged open and out of the rain came a huge jetblack mountain of a man. Must be Junior thought Bodeen. Ella rushed into his wet arms. She barely reached his waist. He lifted her up and kissed her soundly.

"Junebug," she giggled, still in his arms. "This is Melvira Dupree and thats Lucas Bodeen. This is my baby, Junebug."

"Pear to be more like a dragonfly or something to me cousin," said Bodeen.

"Talk to me," roared Junior. "Talk to the Burner. My honey she call me Junior, but most folks call me the Burner, cause I don't leave no trail. My pappy claim I'm half alligator, half snapping turtle, with a little taste of Mississippi bolt lightning thrown in for seasoning. I gits me a little exercise every morning by putting a bend in the river just to hear the steamboat blow."

"Causing me," said Bodeen "to have to straighten out come evening just so the water can flow."

"Talk to me! Talk to the Burner!"

"Junebug you sit down and behave yourself, we got company."

"Yessmam."

He winked at Bodeen. "Tyrants ain't they man? I may be the lightning but Lord knows she thinks she the thunder."

"Junebug!"

"They the company baby, not me, they the ones got to behave theyself." He poked his daughter in her ribs. "Ain't that right Sista?"

Her little oval face lit up with suppressed giggles. She looked at her momma to see if she could laugh at daddy's clowning. He so funny sometimes. Ella okayed it with a smile, and Sista burst into giggles that filled the house. Junebug responded with booming laughter and a loud and rowdy, "Talk to me! Talk to the Burner!"

Ella shook her head at Junebug in mock disapproval and gave Bubba a plate to take to Momma Gerri. The door opened again and the old man came in trailing storm. He sat at the table, laid his shotgun across his lap and started wiping it dry. Ella called the rest of them to the table. They sit and dig in. Ella could seriously burn and the table groaned under a heaping mess of black-eyed peas, cornbread, candied yams, ribs, peach and apple cobbler, rice, greens, biscuits, irish potatoes and beef stew. The rain pounded the roof and Bodeen felt just about as snug and homey as a stranger can. He looked wistfully on all this domestic satisfaction, his ever-watchful eye on Melvira growing fonder by the moment. Good food, good company, a warm fire on a rainy day and Melvira Dupree. If it wasn't Bodeen Heaven it was close enough. He finally pushed himself back and burped without shame. Melvira frowned at him. The savage. He apologized, but it wasn't sincere.

The old woman sat quietly near the fire, food untouched, chair rocking, playing with the roots inside the bowl in her lap.

"So what do you do for a living Bodeen," Junior asked, "sides talk big that is."

"I play a fair to middling blues piano. Dupree here do con . . ." He trailed off when she gave him the "no" look.

Bubba's little moon face lit up. "You play the blues Mr. Bodeen?"

"Bubba say he gon play a guitar on Beale Street when he grow up," said Sista.

"Did not," Bubba shot back, checking out his parents to see how they took this unauthorized information. When they didn't jump him, he got bold about it.

"You play guitar Mr. Bodeen?"

"Fraid not Bubba, I just play piano."

"Is piano better than guitar daddy?"

"Just different son," said Junior, "like folks is different."

"Yall just relax now Bubba," chided Ella, "told you not to bother Mr. Bodeen till he through eating. You want a second helping Mr. Bodeen?"

"Well only if you absolutely insist."

"I insist. Absolutely."

"Talk to me!"

The Burner laughed and smacked the table. "Boy you gon eat my food and steal my lines too?"

Bodeen was the only one still eating. The old man was oiling his shotgun, little black eyes steadily moving from one person to the other. Ella started cleaning the table. Melvira stood to help; Ella shook her head. "No, I believe Momma Gerri wants to talk to you."

Melvira had avoided the old woman's eyes during the meal. She looked now, and Momma Gerri nodded at her. Melvira walked over and sat beside the fire with her back to the wall, relishing the warmth. The headtied woman played with the roots in the wooden bowl, tossed and studied them, patient, unhurried, all the time in the world. Melvira was grateful for the opportunity to just sit there warmed by the fire. Bodeen glanced over. She smiled a reassurance, and he turned back to the meal. Melvira was curiously pleased with the unspoken conversation. Sista came over and curled up in her lap, and Mel instinctively stroked the child's head. Finally the old woman sighed and nodded her satisfaction with the root configuration. The rain pounded the roof and walls, and there was the far-off rumbling thunder of Oluddumare's drum.

The old woman again nodded her satisfaction. "Come morning," she said, "my man will show you the road to Taproot."

Melvira glanced at the old man sitting at the table, oiling the barrel of his shotgun with the steady strokes of a rag. He looked back with hard, impenetrable eyes, and he nodded—the gate would be open.

"Thank you," said Melvira.

The headtied woman settled back into her rocking chair without a reply. Melvira absently stroked the head of the child nestled into the crook of her arm. It was a quiet comfortable moment. Dishes forgot, Junebug and Ella cuddled together in a big chair in front of the fire. Bodeen was still at the table, belly tight, relishing the taste of a solid homecooked meal. Bubba came to stand in front of him.

"So Mr. Bodeen, tell me about the blues."

"Bubba you quit bothering Mr. Bodeen now."

Bodeen grinned at Ella. He wasn't bothered. He liked turning little kids on to the blues. Passing it on.

"Can you really play the blues?" asked Bubba.

"Tell me a story."

Bubba looks confused and disappointed. A story? His expression says that this is interesting but it ain't no blues. Bodeen sang.

Tell me your story and
I will sing you a blues
In the midst of hardtimes
I'll find the good news

Bubba's little eyes lite up, thats better, now we talking blues.

"Well all right," boomed Junior, "talk to me! Talk to the Burner!"

"The blues is about a lot of things," said Bodeen. "The blues about accepting life for what it is, good and bad. Its about making folks feel what you feel. And its mostly about people and life and stories. You know any stories?"

Bubba shook his head.

"Sing me a lovesong bluesman," said Momma Gerri, eyes closed, chair rocking. "You know any love stories?"

Bodeen looked at her. Her eyes opened and something passed between them. He smiled his thanks. A major part of telling stories is knowing which story to tell when.

> *I come a long long way to get to where I am*
> *I've walked naked through the fire and the storm.*

sang Lucas Bodeen, a man who finally understands the nature of love.

> *and the one thing I've learned*
> *is a good woman must be earned*
> *I want to be your man*
> *I'm man enough to keep you warm.*

Late that night, the rest of the house asleep, rain still tattooing the roof, Melvira and Bodeen lay snugly wrapped in a blanket near the glowing embers of the fire. Not quite touching but close enough to feel each other's presence. Bodeen is satisfied. Melvira in his arms again. Well almost in his arms. Close enough that he didn't care how rough it got henceforth. Far as Luke Bodeen was concerned it was strictly blue skies and roses.

"You ever find that blues you were looking for Lucas?"

He shrugged in the darkness. "I don't rightly know, you just work and hope. I just do what I do and do my best. You never know whats gon touch folks, or another bluesman. You put out as many pieces as you can, you let time make the judgment. Had a chance to record but I missed it."

"O no, not a chance to record," she said, knowing what it must have cost him. "Bodeen, how could you? What happened?"

He resisted the impulse to make points. "Something came up."

"More important than recording your blues?"

"Looks like it."

She shifted a heartbeat closer. She may not have realized it but Bodeen did. In every iota of his soul he felt it.

"Howcum you never had any children Melvira?"

Her hand strayed to the redflannel bag she kept tied on a red string around her waist and hanging between her legs. "There're ways."

Her tone didn't invite further question, but Bodeen wanted to know. He thought about Bubba's excitement earlier. Boy might make a good bluesman one day with proper guidance.

"Shoulda maybe asked howcum you don't want any children?"

Pause. A heartbeat. Two.

"Do you have children Bodeen? Any that you lived with, that you raised, that you know?"

Bodeen didn't answer. A little girl in Carolina. Twin boys in Chicago. Probably more. Ain't nothing he can say. One of the legendary missing black fathers. You been a trifling man Lucas Bodeen. He could feel his daddy frowning down on him. Ancestor embarrassment. I'll make it up to em daddy. I swear.

He had taken too long to answer her. Not that it made that much difference. She knew the answer. If it didn't have anything to do with the blues, it really didn't mean much to him. It just wasn't real. He felt her move that same heartbeat's length away.

Sleep, when it finally came, was light and troubled, and he more felt the cry than heard it. He woke confused and disoriented, but the rain drumming on the roof focused him. The mule-drawn wagon, the old man, a warm house full of good people. Breathing irregularly beside him, Melvira tossed fitfully and muttered in her sleep,

"Momma please."

Bodeen pulled her close and stroked her forehead. "Its okay baby, its okay," he whispered. "Its okay. Really."

"Momma please."

She gradually subsided and laid in his arms, breathing regular again, face composed and so pretty in the emberlight. He felt so good lying there holding her, comforting her, feeling so soft and protective, that he didn't move, even when his arm went to sleep or when his manhood rose rampant against her thigh. Just lying there beside her felt as good as making love to some other woman. Better. The one woman in the world that would never bore him. My boy Bodeen is a satisfied man.

A wet delta morning crouched low and waited for them. They almost hated to leave, but the old man was up and obviously waiting when they rose, shotgun still cradled in his arms. "Wonder if he slept with it?" whispered Bodeen. Before she left, she went to the old woman and nodded her thanks again. Momma Gerri looked up and met her eyes for the briefest moment and turned back to the fire, still handling the seven roots in her bowl.

Outside, the rain was drizzling with occasional heavy wind-driven bursts. Bodeen sat in the car behind the old man and his wagon. Sista was standing at the door and Melvira picked her up, hugged her good. Looked fondly on the woman growing inside the child. The little girl put her lips to Melvira's ear. "I know who you are. Momma Gerri told me. When I grow up I'll find you."

She wiggled free and ran inside. Melvira looked after her with a strange longing before grabbing up her skirt and running for the car. Bodeen had the door open and she darted inside. Impulsively, she hugged him. He beamed. Glowed. Even as he wondered, what now? Never will understand this woman.

He started the car. "Listen to that baby purr," he said, talking about the car and looking at her. "The old man ain't much on conversation, but he do appear to have the magic touch. You all right?"

Touching his forearm, she smiled and nodded. Ahead of them, the old man geed up his mule and she nodded Bodeen to follow. He stroked her damp hair, relishing the softness before gearing up and following the rattling wagon through the sporadically heavy rain. Ella and Junebug waved them off. Bodeen hated to leave. They drove along behind the old man, crawling along to match his pace on the wet, muddy road. Bodeen was mighty impatient, but he checked himself. By now he knew that he was in the middle of a hoodoo thing, but as long as he was with Melvira he didn't really care. For a fact, he suspected it might even be a good blues in it. He hummed a few exploratory chords and, feeling good, he absently reached over and stroked her hair back again. And whats more she didn't stop him.

Still following the wagon, they crested a delta hill and came on a wide delta flatland dominated by a huge tree standing on the horizon. The tree stood starkly alone against the flat horizon, inexorably drawing the eye. As they drove toward it slowly, she slid her hand over and began stroking his biceps. A soothing thing. She knew her man.

Bodeen was barely conscious of her stroking hand as the nature of the tree began to dawn on him. The car slowed down to a stop and the still-moving wagon gained ground. Hanging from the tree was fresh delta fruit. A hanged man. A blackman, lynched and burned. Always stay on your guard children. The stories I could tell. The tiny hairs on the back of Bodeen's neck rose and an ancient primal growl rumbled low in his throat. He pulled out his hognose and scanned the empty horizons before climbing down, pistol ready, even eager.

The old man had stopped and sat as impassively as a statute in the rain.

Bodeen walked over to his wagon and looked at him belligerently. "Whats this old man?"

The old man looked at him from eyes shadowed beneath the wide slouch hat. Melvira walked up and laid a calming hand on Bodeen's forearm.

"Which way to Taproot?" she asked.

The old man pointed south at a winding road that went through an open picket fence. "You follow this road south, no matter what, take you straight to Taproot."

"Thank you," said Dupree.

The old man tipped his hat to her and geed his mule. He turned his wagon around and drove back the way they came. Luke Bodeen didn't hardly notice; he was staring at the hanged man, disgusted with himself, the old man and life in the delta. Suddenly so very weary, he walked slowly through the sucking mud to the burnt thing, hanging from the old delta tree and swaying slightly in the delta wind and rain. The body was wet and soggy; it hadn't burnt thoroughly and stank like the half-burnt meat that it was. The muddy ground around it was tracked up and littered with the remains of a delta picnic, broken parasols, wet crumpled paper, beercans and liquor bottles, folding seats. Looks like folk had had a pleasant Sunday morning. A little down-home delta fun.

"Damn em," muttered Bodeen, "damn em all."

He looked at the pistol in his hand like he had forgotten that he was carrying it. Then he emptied his hognose into the trunk of the tree, damning em with every shot.

Melvira waited until the gun was empty, Bodeen still firing on empty chambers, before she gently took it from his hand.

"Hurting the tree," she said, "don't help the man."

"Helped me." His voice was supposed to be angry but sounded dead instead. She stuck the empty gun in the waistband of his pants and began trying to unloosen the wet chains that held the deadman still swaying from the branch. The heavy wet chain was more than she could handle, and Bodeen took over with a vengeance. Handling the deadmeat itself was a challenge that Lucas failed and he vomited all over the halfcooked thing before they finally got it unchained and loose of the tree. He was soaking wet from rain and tears by the time he dug a shallow grave in the soft muddy ground and covered it with rocks from the field. Then he was ready to go and waited impatiently in the car while Melvira said a short prayer over the makeshift grave.

He drove silently past the tree and beyond, eyes strictly on the road, his conversation consisting of one-word replies. His people lived such a hard life. The rain clouded his vision and the bitterness clouded his soul.

"Nothing you can do about it now Lucas," she said, fingering her roots and wondering what she herself would do.

"No. At least I owe him a blues," said Lucas Bodeen, "least we forget."

The rain got bad soon after that, each drop a stinging nail slung sideways by the rain. They found a empty barn as soon as they could, and Bodeen was able to pull his car right up through the big double doors. It was a big relief getting in out of the now-insistent rain. They dried off and collected enough dry hay into a corner to burrow into. Outside the rain beat against the walls of the barn and slipped in through the cracks, but burrowed deep into the warm hay and their red blanket, the faint spray just felt refreshing. Tired and relatively dry, they went straight to sleep.

At some point in the deepest part of the night Melvira rose, vaguely bothered. She reached out with her senses and found nothing wrong. Other than the rain still battering the roof, the barn was quiet. She saw the hanged man again, silhouetted against the evening sky. No, that wasn't what bothered her. She sent forth her traveling spirit, and she saw animals of field and farm, house and woods in communal flight, and she felt the earth trembling in fear. She called back her traveling spirit and shook Bodeen awake.

"Lucas."

"Wha?"

"The river's coming."

Bodeen was instantly awake and listening fiercely. Didn't hear nothing but rain. But if Melvira Dupree said the river was coming, then the river was coming. Right away he's up and he's moving.

"Coming this way?"

She nodded as she threw their blanket in the car. Lucas manhandled the door of the barn open and the storm leaped in at them. Animals ran by as they watched, deer and wolf side by side, wild dog and tame. Bodeen looked at her hopefully and she shook her head no, we got to go.

They climbed in and Bodeen wound her up and they drove out into the hammering rain. For a minute Bodeen didn't know which way to turn, then, instinctively, he followed the rest of the fleeing animals. Struggling to keep the fishtailing car on the wet muddy road, they drove along with a silent determination. Then they heard it, a low rumble growing behind them. The Mississippi coming. Bodeen put the pedal to the metal and, tires spewing mud, the little car leaped through the rain. Behind them the rumbling grew. Holding on as the car swerved wildly down the road, Melvira looked behind them and gasped at a black wall of water, blacker than the night and towering into the sky. The mad mighty Mississippi, kicking ass and taking names. Melvira pulled on Lucas' arm and pointed to a high rounded hill by the side of the road. Bodeen nodded, careened off the road and tried to ram his car up the hill. The tires spun, refusing to grip the muddy ground. The river was rushing them, an angry black wall of water getting closer by the moment. Melvira jumped out of the car and started scrambling up the hill, yelling for Bodeen to follow her. Bodeen was still gunning the motor and spinning his wheels, trying to get his little precious car to traction on up that hill. She turned, screaming into the wind and rain, "Lucas, leave it!"

He spent precious moments scrounging around in the backseat till he found that old crooked broom of his. He jumped out, taking a calm moment to affectionately pat the hood of the little car that he had won with a pair of Jacks and a lot of nerve. And then he was scrambling up the hill one step ahead of the raging Mississippi, boiling and bubbling and talking to him real bad. A couple of times Bodeen almost slid back down into the water for refusing to let go of that broom. It tugged greedily at his ankles as they scampered up and finally out of its angry reach. He looked back and watched his car disappear in a swirl of water and metal as the hungry river swallowed it whole. Gasping for breath and still fighting against the hammering rain, they crawled deep into brush at the top of the hill. They had done all they could. Let the storm do what it will.

Cold bright moonlight woke Lucas Bodeen. It took him a minute to orient himself. Right. Flood. Melvira slept spooned beside him, bedraggled and caked with mud. After the violence of the storm, the quiet night was a loud, hard silence. He disentangled himself carefully, but woke her anyway. Last night could have been dismissed as a dream but for a circle of naked treetops stripped of foliage and a moonlit muddy lake surrounding their little hill like a bright brown mirror. A roof stood forlornly in the distance. All kinds of debris from the storm floated sluggishly by, uprooted trees, lumber, branches, furniture. Bodeen walked to the edge of the hill and looked out over the muddy lake that surrounded them. Melvira came up beside him and started stirring the muddy water clear.

"What you looking for Bodeen?"

"My car."

"Bodeen."

She was pointing out across the black lake. A steamboat. A big double-deck sternwheeler. Steaming up out of the night. Miles from the river. He stood and walked over to the bank.

"Heard about it once before," he said. "During the

flood of 1917, the *Chas P. Organ* crossed on water bout thirty feet deep, picking up folks that were stranded. Can't wait," said Bodeen with a little boy's pleasure, "to tell folks that I saw a riverboat sailing on dry land."

"Ain't exactly dry," she said.

"Close enough," he said, "for me to tell the story that way."

Churning silvery water up behind it, the big riverboat glided through the darkness. They watched it with a curious awe that caused them not to even try to hail it. Bodeen watched it churn along until it was swallowed by the night.

Bodeen turned back. Melvira had pulled her blouse off, first using it to wash herself, then washing it. Her thin shift plastered itself to her body, and Bodeen watched appreciatively. This might not be all that bad after all. Under her shift her breasts shift heavily, the fat nipples that he just loved to finger tracing designs on the thin material. Bodeen's nature commence to rising.

"Forget it Bodeen."

"Hey just tell me 'no.' "

"No."

She finished cleaning herself as best she could and laid her wet blouse out to dry. Bodeen pulled his broom out of the brush and washed it in the dirty water.

"Spec a boat be along sooner or later," he said, obviously unconcerned.

"Lucas, don't you ever give up?"

He walked over, crowding her, patience lost to the soft moonlight on a muddy brown lake.

"Told you a long time ago I ain't gon never let you go Melvira."

He tried to make it light and joking, putting his arms around her and gently trying to pull her to him. She stiffened and drew back.

"Lucas."

"Aw Melvira, how long you gon punish me?"

"It's not punishment Bodeen, I just don't feel what you do."

"Baby I've missed you so much. You just don't know. Don't you understand how much I love you? Everything I do is a lovesong for you."

"Bodeen, please . . ."

Her voice gave nothing. In fact, she sounded irritated. Pissed. Exasperated. Bodeen stepped back. There is like this click inside him and he's through. He's remembering all the begging he did that last year in Memphis. This has gone on long enough. He searched her face in the moonlight, trying to see what he's been missing. If there was anything there, seems like she would know by now. She was too serious a woman to be playing with him, and he was too serious a man to keep begging for love.

"Aw hell Melvira, why you let me go this far if you still saying 'no.'"

"I said 'no' when we left Memphis Lucas, I been saying 'no' all this time."

"I know you said 'no,' but I didn't think you meant 'no.'"

Her expression said that I always mean what I say, those old familiar rigid lines digging deep proud grooves around her mouth.

And its like he's seeing for the first time. Begging for love just did not strike him as the behavior of a serious man.

"You just don't understand do you?" he said finally, not even angry any more, just sorry he's wasted so much of his life on this. How dare she call those puny calculated passions of hers love. Then again, he thought, maybe its me who don't understand.

"Did you ever love me?" he asked, and was immediately sorry. Just how long you gon beg boy. He felt like a fool. She couldn't love him. Not like he loved her. The way he feels about her nothing else in the world mattered. Nothing. Well Luke Bodeen wasn't going to play her fool anymore. He looked around the night, impatient now with her company.

"Bodeen you left . . ."

"Yeah, yeah," he held his hand up, "I know. Forget I asked. You too hard on me Melvira, and I been singing this duet solo too long."

"Bodeen, cant we be just friends?"

He was standing there looking at her, wanting her so bad he could hardly breathe.

"No," he said, genuinely sorry. "No we can't."

He walked over to the other side of the hill and sat facing the water.

She watched him. Maybe she was being foolish. But she was afraid that if she let herself go he'd just hurt her again. All or nothing is all she knows, and she doesn't trust him or herself enough to give Lucas Bodeen her all. She composed herself and waited for the boat to come.

Bodeen laid on his back, hands behind his head, watching the stars in the night sky and listening to the moan of a nightwind that sounded like it felt just like he did. And then again, in a way he's kinda relieved. Maybe now he would be truly free of her. He had had to try this one last time, couldn't have lived with himself without trying. Well he had shot his best shot and he missed. So—what was he going to do now? See her to Taproot, like he said he would. Then maybe go down to New Orleans and see what was happening with this Jass thing. There were a couple of women in New Orleans who would be pleased to see him. Be a nice change to spend some time with a woman who liked him. Wonder what they were doing up in Harlem these days. Couldn't be much if they were doing it without him. You know, there were still a few things to be said for being a free man.

He wasn't aware of falling asleep until she woke him. It was still night and the moon was low in the sky.

"Bodeen, a boat."

A small rowboat off in the distance moving aimlessly in the sluggish current.

"Aw hell Melvira, its just a dinky little rowboat and its too far away. We can wait till we get picked up."

"Now, we got to go. You got a fever coming and what I need to break it ain't here."

Fever? He felt his forehead. Didn't feel a thing. Didn't feel bad either. He made an impatient sound and started to go back to sleep.

"Bodeen!"

Melvira had her dress hitched up around her hips

and was already wading into the water. Bodeen ain't moved.

"Bodeen."

"Hell woman," he said, not feeling very cooperative, "its too damned far away. I don't see why we don't just wait to get got. Somebody be along directly with a real boat. You ain't in that big a hurry are you? You ain't got to worry none about me bothering you, if thats your problem."

She was already in the water up to her knees.

"Bodeen!"

He irritably sucked a tooth, but he got on up. Might as well get it over with. He picked up the crooked old broom he had saved from the flood, carried it to the bank and threw it into the river. Watched it float away till the waterlogged straws drug it under.

"Bodeen! Come on."

He trudged over like a little boy being made to take a bath. He ventured a few cautious steps into the muddy water, peering intently into it and muttering to himself that he couldn't see where he was stepping. He was clearly concerned about snakes. Now if you know the Mississippi River you know its naturally muddy, too thick to drink and too thin to plow. But when it floods, its damn near solid mud. Godzilla could be hid off in there and you wouldn't know it.

"Bodeen!"

Okay, she was pissing him off now. Snakes or not, he waded into the water without any further ado. "I'm coming," he snarled. "Quicker we get this over with the quicker I can be on my way."

He started swimming with solid determined strokes until he reached the boat and pulled himself in. Inside he found a broken paddle and used it to paddle over to the still swimming Dupree, but he didn't help her in. He just sat there and watched her work herself into the boat.

"No need to be petty Bodeen. You asked to come remember? I didn't ask you."

Bodeen starts paddling. Due south.

"Petty ain't all I'm gon be," he said flatly. "Soon as I get you to Taproot I'm gon be gone. I've given this foolishness all its going to get from me."

And this time he meant it. Luke Bodeen was through begging for love. He paddled through the moonlit night with a vengeance, soon falling into the rhythm of his stroke. Next thing he knows he's waking up and he's lying in this big four-poster featherbed under a thick pink comforter and a big pink canopy overhead. Furthermore, he was apparently surrounded by about 12, 13 exquisite women of all shapes and shades, dressed and undressed in an array of frilly lingerie. Must be dreaming. He closed his eyes and opened them again. They were still there.

Must be heaven, he thought. He had always wondered if there was pussy after death.

"Heaven?" he asked tentatively. At the sound from him the women started chattering like a flock of disturbed birds. They spooked him.

"Melvira?"

She leaned into his range of vision and placed a cool towel on his brow.

"Here I am Bodeen."

He sighed relief before he remembered that he was through with her.

"Where's here?"

"Town cathouse, and the best bed I could find while I was breaking your fever."

Fever? Now that she mentioned it he did feel kinda weak and fuzzy. He had thought it was all these pretty gals had him dizzy. A couple of the working women flirted with him, smiles, winks and twitching red lips. He winked back at a fetching young redbone that particularly caught his eye. Ol' Bodeen was beginning to appreciate the situation. This ain't bad, he thinking. Ain't bad atall.

"How long I been out?"

Melvira held out a bowl of some kind of gruel. She dipped a big spoonful and tried to get him to take it.

"Three days. Here, you need to eat this."

Maybe so, but all these fine, attentive women were reminding him of unfinished business. Fighting off dizziness, he pushed the spoon to the side and swung himself from under the covers and out of the bed. Butt naked. The ladies squealed, fluttered and applauded as the rather well-endowed Lucas Bodeen stood, took the bowl in both hands and turned it up to his mouth. Still dizzy and swaying, he drained it and waited for the room to stop spinning. Then he bowed with the utmost dignity to the still-clapping women, reached for the clothes laid out beside the bed and began dressing.

"You ain't ready for traveling yet Bodeen," said Melvira perfunctorily, knowing he was in no mood to listen. "You need your rest."

"I need to get you to Taproot and be on my way, thats

what I need. I've already wasted five years of my life on you woman and I ain't got no more time to give you. I'ma get you to Taproot and let your momma have you. I pity the woman. If she had any sense she woulda stayed gone."

The wagonload of pigs pulled over to the side of the road and stopped.

"This is it yall," the grizzled old farmer up front yelled back at them. Melvira and Bodeen climbed down from the back of the wagon and looked around.

"This is what?" muttered Bodeen.

Wasn't nothing but trees, bush and winding delta road, but there was the stream and the little bridge. Melvira recognized them from the journey of her traveling spirit.

"Why Taproot Mississippi son" said the pigman, tugging at the straps of his overalls. "Course there ain't much of it, never was. Couple of folks cross the bridge there. Thats about it."

He pointed out the small wooden bridge crossing the stream. He addressed himself to Bodeen, but Bodeen still had a attitude and hadn't said more than This is what? since they left the whorehouse and flagged the pigwagon down.

The pigman shrugged it off. The boy's bad manners wasn't no concern of his. "Hope you didn't rile my hogs with your funky attitude boy," said the pigman, gigging up his horse and pulling off. "Grumpy hogs brings they price down."

Melvira had already started off cross the bridge. Lucas tagged along, with her and not with her. They walked into the heavily misted woods aways, Melvira leading the way with a false confidence as the path became less and less a path and more and more woods. Now that she had reached the end of her journey she questioned it. She hoped her mother was here, and then again she didn't. What does she want, why did she come? How would she treat the woman? How would her . . . no, the woman, treat her? The deeper they got into the Taproot Woods the more the mist and her anxieties seemed to thicken. And then in the distance they heard a passing train call out. Bodeen stopped and listened.

"That your train?" she asked coldly, grateful for something to turn her anxieties on. "You don't have to come if you don't want to Bodeen."

He shrugged. Luke Bodeen was a Tennessee boy. A southern gentleman. Ain't no woman ever going to be able to say that Luke Bodeen was a trifling man. It was his understanding that you always saw a lady to her door.

"Don't worry about me. You worry about that cabin over there."

He pointed. She was startled; she hadn't realized they were that close. A small lowbuilt cabin surrounded by misted shadows that appeared to grow thicker even as they watched. It seemed deserted except for a frizzy-combed rooster pecking his way about in the front yard. A big crow rose gracefully out of the woods in front of them, and they watched it climb effortlessly into the sky.

Then it cawed, and the trees around them began rustling and the sun was suddenly blotted as hundreds of crows rose cawing from the trees. The sound of their flapping wings was deafening and their numbers darkened the sky. Another caw and the skyful of crows began converging on them. Dupree was fascinated and just stood there watching them, but Bodeen freaked. He grabbed her arm and, half dragging her, ran for the cabin door. The crows were almost on them when suddenly a clear yet ineffably old voice came from inside.

"Melvira? That you baby?"

At the sound of the little voice like a tiny bell ringing, the diving crows veered off and settled back into the woods around them. The sky cleared and the rustling trees grew gradually faint until the woods were again still and silent. Melvira stared at the door from which the voice had come. Bodeen was staring suspiciously at the now quiet woods. He checked his derby for bird droppings.

The voice from inside, "That you baby?"

Melvira started toward the door. Bodeen didn't move. Hand on the door, she turned to look back at him. He raised his hand "goodbye." A sad little gesture.

"Just don't feel like singing no more solo lovesongs baby. You take care of yourself now."

He turned and walked into the woods, glancing occasionally into the trees but never back. Melvira stood with her heart in her throat. Try once more Lucas. She opened her mouth and closed it.

"Melvira."

She pushed open the door. Inside the cabin is spotless, naked of everything but a wooden pallet laying on the floor in a corner and a brand-new broom standing behind the door. The little old lady lying there under colorful patchwork quilts peered up from one uncovered eye. Even old, sick and obviously tired like only the really old can be, she radiated a presence that Melvira felt the moment she walked in the room. It didn't take a hoodoo to see that she was dying.

"Shouldna ought to let him go, cant be scared of life daughter."

Now I don't think that there is anything the old lady could have said that would have infuriated Melvira Dupree more. After all these years, and her mother's first words were a lecture. Years of locked-up anger made her cold. She walked over to the pallet and looked down through hooded eyes on the little woman lying there. Angry yet curious eyes. What was it about this woman that had left myth and legend in her life's wake? All she saw was this frail little woman, face deeply wrinkled and even more deeply lived, staring evenly back at her through one redrimmed eye. Melvira Dupree looked to see if she could see herself there. She did. And felt nothing. And that was good.

"What do you want? Why have you called me here?" Her voice was steady. No beg, no whine, no love, not even hate. And that too was good.

"Wondered if you were going to make it in time." Struggling to sit up in the bed, she reached out a thick-veined hand, and Melvira stepped out of her reach. Spent, the old woman slowly lowered herself back down to the pallet, collecting breath and energy for her next effort.

"What do you want?"

Melvira knew she lessened herself, but she wanted

to hurt as she has been hurt. Effie chuckled, but the sound didn't reach the one eye that stared at her daughter. "Guess I cant expect any different from you."

"I guess you can't."

That she was dying was clear, but Melvira didn't care. She has found her. They have spoken. There was no reason to stay. There was no mystery here.

"Damn you," said Melvira, "for the rest of your days, however few they may be." She turned to walk away.

"Come back here!"

The voice of command. Melvira spun and snarled, "You don't have the right to talk to me like that."

"I talk to you any damn way I please."

Effie Dupree sat up in the bed, infirmity forgotten, her one eye glaring. What Melvira saw of herself in the feisty old woman just made her angrier.

"You got nothing to say about my life, or what I do with it. Suddenly after all these years you want to play momma." And then, surprising them both, her voice cracked. "Why . . . why did you leave me?"

The old woman saw her daughter's pain and knew it as her own. She had much to answer for. She had known it would be difficult to know her daughter, but even she had not expected the intensity of Melvira's resentment. She lowered herself back to the bed, spent, suddenly nothing but a tired old woman, whatever it was that had been keeping her strong seeping from her under her daughter's hard and unforgiving eyes. She had never in her life said she was sorry about anything, didn't know how, but she tried. "I had a plan baby, I . . ."

"Don't call me baby," Melvira spat at her.

The old woman flinched.

"Why?" snapped Melvira.

Melvira didn't really want an answer, she just wanted to hurt, to prove to herself somehow that her mother cared. Yet when she drew blood it merely fed her anger. She withheld the forgiveness her mother wanted and needed with a vengeance, glad to have such a weapon at her disposal.

"Why!"

Everytime she barked it, the little old woman flinched.

"Why?"

Effie Dupree almost smiled under her pain. Much as it hurt, still her daughter was there and she was all that Effie Dupree could have ever hoped that she would be. But was it worth it? No. She's missed too much. No. Nothing was worth the pain her baby carried. She's made a mistake that will feed on itself for generations. But she is too much the professional to let awareness of a lifemistake break her at this point of the game. She has survived the unsurvivable before.

A knock on the door. Sharp and authoritative. Effie sighed, whats done is done. She nodded Melvira to the door. Melvira hesitated just enough to let the woman know that she doesn't take orders.

The Baron, standing there, respectfully, hat in hand. Behind him, a setting sun takes the light from the western sky. The rooster in the yard crowed.

The Baron's voice is like a dry distant wind.

"Evening Miz Dupree. I come to see your momma."

"No."

The crooked old man is reasonable. "Now look Miz Dupree, I . . ."

"Leave!" said Melvira Dupree. "You have no business here. Leave, I command it."

In spite of himself the crooked old man stepped back. Then he caught himself and his face hardened.

From the pallet, Effie chuckled with pleasure. "Don't be like that daughter. Melvira." As though she likes the sound of the word in her mouth, she repeats it, "Melvira. My baby. Let the man in, I been expecting him."

Melvira stood in his way, throbbing with power, unwilling to give an inch. Not this time. By the gods no.

"Please baby," Effie Dupree said softly. "I'm tired. I'm weary. In my bones I'm weary."

Body jerking as if under control of another, Melvira stood aside. The crooked old man entered and nodded graciously.

"Thank you Miz Dupree. How do Effie?"

"I'll take tolerable . . . all things considered."

They spoke like old friends. The Baron moved toward the pallet, and Melvira once again stepped forward, her voice throbbing with power.

"No!"

The Baron whimpered and stumbled, paling under his dark skin.

"Melvira!" snapped Effie Dupree. Melvira dropped her head and stepped back.

"Momma," she whimpered, a word so soft.

Effie Dupree motioned her daughter over to her. Melvira walked over woodenly.

"Baby I'm tired. I called out to you because I didn't

want my spirit roaming unclaimed. Ain't nothing I can say to you about why I left thats gon convince you. All I can do is ask your forgiveness. I know now that you all I got. All I ever had."

"You are my ancestor," said Melvira Dupree, in the solemn monotone of ritual, "and I have found you." A tear gathered in the corner of her eye. Effie put out the same thickly veined hand that caused her daughter to jerk away earlier and captured it. The gift of tears. She used the finger to stroke the patched socket of the eye that she left in Sweetwater Arkansas. "I watched over you best I could," she said, "and I'll be even closer now."

The effort obviously tired her and she faded for a moment, becoming o so beautiful as her spirit began to rise to the surface of the dying fleshy envelope and fill the room with a soft and brilliant light.

"Momma," Melvira whimpered.

Effie closed her good eye and a divine luminescence grew. Melvira refused to move away, and the crooked old man had to step around her. He took the soul. Without the driving force that had animated it so fiercely, the shell appeared to shrink into itself, the one eye still open. Melvira fell limply to her knees beside the bed.

The crooked old man stepped around her and stopped at the door. "She was a good woman, you needn't worry about her. Good day to you Miz Dupree."

He left her there. After awhile she reached out and closed the staring eye. Rest momma.

Morning rose and found her unmoved.

Again a knock on the door, this time hesitant and unsure, life is far more timid than death. Melvira didn't answer, and the door was slowly pushed open. Luke Bodeen of course, smiling with a rueful resignation.

"What can I say girl," he said sheepishly. "So I'm a fool for you, so what else is new."

Then he saw the body and the new lines of pain etched into her face.

"Oh baby. Oh baby."

He gathered her into his arms. The dam loosened and, burrowing into his chest, she broke down in deep tormented sobs that finally released a lifetime of pain.

Geas

I lay

on me and mine

Guidance

They buried Effie Dupree in her garden. Under a bright setting sun haloed in orange shades of sky.

"Where to now Melvira? You staying here?"

"I don't think so."

Bodeen cleared his throat.

"I been thinking about going down to New Orleans, see what they doing with this Jass thing. Last time I was down there they were calling it Jazz."

Melvira scraped a shallow hole into Effie's grave with her fingers and put Hoodoo Maggie's mojohand in it. She savored Effie's approval. Yes, I know momma.

The ancestors approve. She does well doesn't she? She does us proud.

Bodeen, not getting a response to his first thrust, tried another.

"They tell me that there is this woman down in New Orleans that supposed to do good hoodoo. Nama Marie Leveaux or something like that, spose to be a hundred years old almost. She suppose to be bad Melvira, real bad."

"Phwwwt, she ain't that bad."

"Folks down that way claim she is."

Melvira looked at him with this deep and affectionate smile. Bodeen tried to look innocent.

"Spec I wouldn't mind seeing a little of the world fore we go back to Memphis," she said.

The music was back in her voice. She was singing at him again, her voice filled with sweet promise. Gloriana hallelujah.

"Baby," he said, his hungry arms opening. She moved into them like flowing water. And Lucas Bodeen is a complete man again. Baby I love you so. Never before has mortal man loved a woman like I love you.

"I'm told Mississippi riverwater is good for growing things," she murmured into his chest.

"Hey," he said, grinning, "I almost forgot."

He went back inside the cabin and came out with the brand-new broom that had stood behind the door. He laid it down crosswise in front of them.

"I don't ever want to lose you again," he said. "I wanna be a married man."

"This ain't no preacher Bodeen."

"We'll do that too, but this means even more to me. My folks did it like this, my granfolks too. They stayed together forever and thats what I wanna be, your man forever. Come on and jump the broom with me Melvira Dupree."

He held out his hand. She took it and they jumped the broom. Laughing, giggling and deliriously happy.

A crow flew out of a tree to Melvira's shoulder and sat there, head curiously cocked to one side. Melvira stroked blueblack feathers.

"You did say didn't you," she asked him, "they did good conjure down there in Brazil?"

"Don't know how good it is, but they do it. A lot of it."

She left the broom standing up on her momma's grave and they walked off into the woods.

"You know Melvira . . ."

"Whats that Bodeen?"

". . . A good woman sure do work a man hard."

"No harder," she replied, "than a good man work a woman."

And on that progressive note they walked hand in hand off into the wooded sunset. I'm told they made a good team, I'm told they made a good life together. Now I'm not saying they didn't have their share of life's little trials and tribulations, and your definition of happy may be different from mine, or theirs, but my understanding is that Melvira Dupree and Lucas Bodeen found the good thing.

And they lived happily ever after.

The end.

Such is my myth

and so it is written

I have spoken

Now it is so

That is all